"Well, well. Lo

Tate squinted into th
that Molly O'Dare, big as life and twice as
exasperating, sat in his leather-seated rocker.
Without saying anything, he held back the
covers so she could climb into bed with him
where she belonged.

"Fat chance," she muttered.

"Then, if you don't mind me asking, what the hell
are you doing in my bedroom at—" he paused to
peer at the bedside clock "—two in the morning?"

Molly crossed her beautiful legs and folded her
hands. "I've got…news, I guess you could say."

Tate felt the cold kiss of dread at his cheek and a
kind of creepy hollow feeling in the pit of his
stomach. If Molly had news for him, it probably
wouldn't be good…. "Spit it out."

And that was just what she did. "I'm pregnant,
Tate Bravo. Sometime next January, you're going
to be a dad…."

And that was it. Before Tate could collect his
wits and stop her, she turned, threw a slim leg
up over the sill and slipped out the window
the way she had come.

Dear Reader,

It's October, the time of year when crisper temperatures and waning daylight turns our attention to more indoor pursuits—such as reading! And we at Silhouette Special Edition are happy to supply you with the material. We begin with *Marrying Molly,* the next in bestselling author Christine Rimmer's BRAVO FAMILY TIES series. A small-town mayor who swore she'd break the family tradition of becoming a mother *before* she becomes a wife finds herself nonetheless in the very same predicament. And the father-to-be? The very man who's out to get her job....

THE PARKS EMPIRE series continues with Lois Faye Dyer's *The Prince's Bride,* in which a wedding planner called on to plan the wedding of an exotic prince learns that *she's* the bride-to-be! Next, in *The Devil You Know,* Laurie Paige continues her popular SEVEN DEVILS miniseries with the story of a woman determined to turn her marriage of convenience into the real thing. Patricia Kay begins her miniseries THE HATHAWAYS OF MORGAN CREEK, the story of a Texas baking dynasty (that's right, *baking!*), with *Nanny in Hiding,* in which a young mother on the run from her abusive ex seeks shelter in the home of Bryce Hathaway—and finds so much more. In *Wrong Twin, Right Man* by Laurie Campbell, a man who feels he failed his late wife terribly gets another chance to make it up—to her twin sister. At least he *thinks* she's her twin.... And in Wendy Warren's *Making Babies,* a newly divorced woman whose ex-husband denied her the baby she always wanted, finds a willing candidate—in the guilt-ridden lawyer who represented the creep in his divorce!

Enjoy all six of these reads, and come back again next month to see what's up in Silhouette Special Edition.

Take care,

Gail Chasan
Senior Editor

Please address questions and book requests to:
Silhouette Reader Service
U.S.: 3010 Walden Ave., P.O. Box 1325, Buffalo, NY 14269
Canadian: P.O. Box 609, Fort Erie, Ont. L2A 5X3

Christine Rimmer

MARRYING MOLLY

Silhouette

SPECIAL EDITION

Published by Silhouette Books

America's Publisher of Contemporary Romance

For those of you who follow the Bravos,
here they are, Texas-style!

 SILHOUETTE BOOKS

ISBN 0-373-24639-0

MARRYING MOLLY

Visit Silhouette Books at www.eHarlequin.com

Printed in U.S.A.

CHRISTINE RIMMER

came to her profession the long way around. Before settling down to write about the magic of romance, she'd been everything from an actress to a phone sales representative to a playwright. Christine is grateful not only for the joy she finds in writing, but for what waits when the day's work is through: a man she loves, who loves her right back, and the privilege of watching their children grow and change day to day. She lives with her family in Oklahoma. Visit Christine at her new home on the Web at www.christinerimmer.com.

THE BRAVOS: HEROES, HEROINES AND THEIR STORIES

Chapter One

"Tate. Wake up, Tate."

Sound asleep, Tate Bravo heard the taunting whisper. He knew the voice. Molly. Damn her. What right did she have to come creeping into his dreams?

And why so often? Seemed like not a night went by that she didn't appear to torment him.

"Hey. Pssst. Tate…"

With a groan, Tate pulled a pillow over his head. "Go 'way, Molly," he muttered, still half-asleep. "Get outta my dreams…"

"Tate Bravo, wake up."

Tate opened his eyes under the pillow. He blinked. "Molly?" He tossed the pillow away and sat up. The window opposite the foot of the bed was open, letting in the warm wind from outside. And Molly O'Dare sat in the leather-seated rocker in the corner, not far from that open window.

"Huh?" Tate squinted into the darkness, still not quite believing it could really be her. But it was. Molly O'Dare, big as life and twice as exasperating. Even through the shadows, with all her clothes on, he knew the shape of her and couldn't mistake the wheat-gold gleam to her hair or the velvety curve of her baby-soft cheek. Her perfume came to him on the night breeze; flowers and musk all mingled together in a scent that seemed specifically created to drive a man wild.

Tate indulged in a slow, knowing smile. "Well, well. Look who's here." He thought a few things he had the good sense not to say. Things like, *Couldn't stay away, could you?* and *I knew you'd be back.*

But no. He wasn't going to gloat, at least not out loud. He'd missed having her warm, soft body beside him in bed. Missed it a lot—much more than he ever intended to let her know. Now that she was finally here, he wasn't doing anything to send her off in a snit.

Keeping his mouth firmly shut, he helpfully held back the covers so she could climb in bed with him where she belonged.

"Fat chance," she muttered. Her tone was not the least bit lustful.

Irritation borne of frustrated desire sizzled beneath his skin. But he didn't let her rile him. Not this time. Calm as you please, he gave her a shrug and tucked the blanket back in place. "Then if you don't mind my asking, what the hell are you doing in my bedroom at—" he paused to peer at the bedside clock "—two in the morning?"

Molly, in a short skirt and a tight-fitting white top

that seemed to gleam in the darkness, rocked back in the chair. She crossed those beautiful legs and folded her hands in her lap. ''I've got…news, I guess you could say.''

Though he was known to be tougher than a basket of snakes, at that moment, Tate Bravo felt the cold kiss of dread at his cheek and a kind of creepy hollow feeling in the pit of his stomach. If Molly had news for him, it probably wouldn't be good.

Tate speared his fingers through his sleep-scrambled hair and let out a low growl of pure suspicion. Why the hell was she here? His best guess, being as how a little hot sex seemed ruled out, was that she must have come up with some new way to rescue the needy—at great expense to the town coffers, of course.

As he had a million times in the past six months, Tate cursed the day Molly managed to get herself elected mayor of *his* town. It was the women who'd done it. They all hung out at Molly's beauty shop. When she'd decided to run for mayor, they rallied around her, making it possible for her to claim fifty-four percent of the vote.

If you asked Tate, Molly's mayorship had been a disaster from the get-go. To Tate's mind—and to the minds of every other red-blooded businessman and responsible citizen in town—Molly O'Dare had been the worst thing to happen to Tate's Junction, Texas, since a disgruntled contingent of Comanche warriors on the run from the Oklahoma reservation took over the place for three days back in 1886.

It was a problem of comprehension, Tate thought. Molly refused to comprehend the way things worked.

She insisted on thinking independently. A very bad choice, as everyone knew that the job of mayor required no thinking at all. It was so simple. Tate Bravo, like his grandfather before him, decided what needed doing. Tate informed the mayor and the town council. They voted as per his instructions. And Tate got what he wanted for the town's betterment.

It had always been done that way.

Until Molly.

From her first town council meeting, Molly refused to do things the way they'd always been done. Molly thought independently and came up with a lot of very bad ideas. When Tate wanted a bond issue, she wanted a sales tax increase. When Tate proposed a plan to improve parking access on Center Street, Molly fought him tooth and nail. Making it easier for the townsfolk to spend money on Center Street could wait, she said, brown eyes flashing, those gorgeous full breasts of hers stuck out high and proud. Oh, no, she'd insisted. Top priority should be putting her plan in place for indigent and shut-in care.

Truth was, Tate had his head screwed on straight when it came to what was best for the Junction—and Molly didn't. Sure, he was all for helping out the needy. But the priority had to be supporting what kept any town running: business and commerce. Molly, a businesswoman herself, ought to have known that. But as mayor, she'd been all heart and no sense, and that was a plain fact.

Tate had been seething with fury since the day she won that damned election. And since their constant head-butting struck sparks in more ways than one, he'd also burned to get her into bed.

And he *did* get her into bed—a few months back. For a marvelous and thoroughly stimulating three weeks, that ripe, lush body of hers was his. In bed, he ruled her. However, once on her feet and wearing her clothes, Molly O'Dare continued to be the usual sharp thorn in his side.

Tate leaned forward a little, straining to see her better. No doubt about it. Tonight, those amber-brown eyes had a strange light in them—determined and angry at the same time. Not good.

"I have debated," she continued bleakly, "debated for a couple of weeks now, whether to tell you this. I don't *want* to tell you this. But I can't see any way around it in the end, being as how this is not something that I plan to hide. And since you're bound to know eventually, I've decided you might just as well know sooner as later. You can start getting used to it. You can start figuring out how you plan to deal with it—because, one way or another, you *are* going to be dealing with it."

Tate dragged himself back against the hand-hammered copper inlay of his bed's massive headboard and reached over to switch on the lamp. In the golden spill of light it provided, he could see the sneer on her soft mouth and the dark circles under those pretty eyes. Something warm and uneasy curled through him. It might have been concern for her. She really didn't look right.

What the hell was going on? "Spit it out," he commanded.

And that was just what she did. "I'm pregnant, Tate Bravo. Over two months along. Sometime next January, you're going to be a dad." She stood, leaving the rocker pitching back and forth behind her. "Your mouth is hanging open," she said.

And that was it. Before Tate could collect his scattered wits and stop her, she turned, threw a slim leg up over the sill and slipped out the window the way she had come.

Chapter Two

"Molly, sweetie, don't you get those scissors near me with your eyes all glazed over like that."

Molly blinked. She glanced at the scissors in her hand and then into the mirror, where she met the wary eyes of Betty Stoops. Red-haired and stick-skinny, Betty sat caped and shampooed in Molly's styling chair, ready for her monthly cut. "Sorry, Betty. Just thinking..."

About Tate Bravo, of course. Molly was feeling a tad guilty over the way she'd handled things the night before.

Okay, so maybe sneaking in through his bedroom window, delivering the big news and then jumping back out the window again hadn't been the most tactful approach to the problem. But she *had* said what needed saying. Discussion of the whole mess could wait.

Molly began snipping at Betty's thinning hair. "So now, how has Titus been doing?"

Betty made a low, fretful sound. "Molly, hon, I cannot tell you. I cannot describe…" Betty launched into a blow-by-blow of her husband's various medical conditions.

I was right to get out when I did last night, Molly silently reassured herself as Betty chattered away. Once Tate got over the shock, there was just no telling what kinds of things he might have said to her—from questioning whether the baby was really his to calling her ugly names to accusing her of trying to trap him into marriage.

Uh-uh. Getting the news out had been about all she could manage for one night. Later for the part with the hollering, the accusations and the recriminations. Later still for working out how much of a role—if any—he would be playing in *her* baby's life.

"I was thinking not quite so much off the sides this time," Betty suggested, eyeing her own reflection appraisingly, turning her head this way and that.

Molly stepped back and assessed the situation. "Sure," she said after a moment. "We can do that."

Molly trimmed and shaped and wondered for about the millionth time what could be the matter with her. How in the world could she have slept with Tate Bravo—repeatedly? And beyond that, how could she have *liked* it so much?

Worst of all, why couldn't she stop dreaming of sleeping with him some more?

Especially now, when she knew for certain that those secret nights in Tate Bravo's bed had produced the typical result.

Pregnant, she thought, in utter disgust. *Knocked up. In Trouble.*

It was the one thing Molly had always sworn was never going to happen to her. And for so long, it hadn't. The past few years, she'd dared to start letting herself believe that she was safe from ending up like her mom—and her Granny Dusty—before her.

She only had one weakness, after all, and that was the fatheaded, far-too-handsome man's man, Tate Bravo. She'd had a hopeless secret crush on Tate for most of her life. But her weakness wasn't supposed to be a problem, as Tate never seemed to know she existed.

But then she got it in her mind to improve a few things in town. She ran for mayor. Once she got elected, Tate knew she existed, all right.

Molly had been sworn in as mayor six months ago, at the first of the year. She and Tate fought tooth and nail through three town council meetings: January, February and March. Then he asked her to dinner— just the two of them, in the massive formal dining room out at the big house on his family's ranch, the Double T. Tate said they would discuss ways to "work together to get things done for our town."

There hadn't been much discussing that night. They barely made it past the appetizer. He was on her like paint, and she didn't complain. She fell right into his bed. Heck. Fell? She jumped in and dragged him in after her. All the years without anything remotely re-sembling a sex life, all those years of forbidden fan-tasies featuring Tate, had caught up with her.

And now she was pregnant.

A woman like Molly knew she had to face facts.

She was thirty years old. Until Tate, there'd been no one. She had no reason to assume there would be someone *after* Tate. This might end up being her only chance to become a mom.

So she was stuck. She refused to throw her one chance at motherhood away, no matter what Tate Bravo might imagine he had to say about it. And she wasn't leaving her salon, Prime Cut, *or* the small Texas town that she loved.

So there she was, just like her mom and her Granny before her—pregnant with no husband in the town where she grew up. Once she started showing, tongues would be wagging. Like grandmother, like mother, like daughter, they would all say.

Well, too bad. She would deal with the gossip when the time came. She was keeping her baby and that was that.

"Molly, did you hear a single word I said?" Betty demanded.

Molly met Betty's eyes again. "I certainly did. That poor Titus. How does he bear up?"

Betty kind of squinted at her. "You know, honey, you don't look all that well."

"Oh, I'm fine," Molly replied, faking lightheartedness for all she was worth. "Never felt better..."

Betty wiggled her drawn-on eyebrows and scowled. "You're not letting that Tate Bravo get you down, are you? Heard he shouted at you last Thursday at the town council meeting..."

Molly's heart did a forward roll and then slammed into her rib cage. Did Betty *know?*

As soon as she thought the question, she rejected it. No one knew—not yet, anyway. By mutual agreement, she and Tate had kept their affair strictly secret. He didn't want the word getting out that he was sleeping with the woman who fought him tooth and nail at every turn. And she didn't want the people who counted on her to find out she couldn't keep her hands off the man who stood for everything that needed changing in their town.

Molly put on a totally unconcerned expression as she combed and then smoothed a section of Betty's hair between two fingers. Neatly, she snipped it even. "Don't you worry, Betty. I can handle Tate Bravo." Oh, and hadn't she just? She'd handled him in ways that would turn Betty's face as red as her hair.

Betty harrumphed. "Well, of course you can. That's why we voted you in as our mayor. It's about time someone stood up to those Tates."

Though Tate's last name was Bravo, his mother had been the only child of the last surviving male Tate. So Tate and his younger brother, Tucker, inherited the extensive Tate holdings when their mother passed away. No one ever talked much about the mysterious man named Bravo who had—according to Tate's mother—married her and sired both her boys. To everyone in town, Tucker and Tate were Tates in the truest sense of the word. And Tates had been running Tate's Junction since the town was named after the first Tucker Tate, way back in 1884.

"We do admire your gumption, Molly."

"Why, thank you, Betty." Molly set down her scissors and grabbed the blow-dryer off the rack where it waited next to a row of curling irons. "Let's just blow you dry, now, shall we?"

* * *

Betty wasn't the only customer to notice Molly's distraction. All day long it was, "Molly, you look worried, girl. What's the matter?" and, "Earth to Molly. Are you in there, doll?" or, "Molly, sweet-heart, what is botherin' you?"

She told each and every one of them that she was fine, perfect, never been better—while the whole time the hard knot in her stomach seemed to promise that any second now Tate would come storming through the shop door and start shouting at her. By six, when she closed up shop, she was a wreck. All she wanted was to crawl into bed with the blinds drawn and a cool cloth over her eyes.

Molly's little bungalow on Bluebonnet Lane was her pride and joy. Sure, it was small—750 square feet, two tiny bedrooms, simple box floor plan—but it was hers and that was what mattered. It sat back from the street surrounded by sweetgums and oaks. On the south end of town, in an area not very developed yet, all tucked into the trees the way it was, the house almost gave a person the feeling she was out in the country.

Molly put her pickup under the carport east of the house. She strolled across the yard to the porch, feel-ing the tensions of the day drain away from between her shoulder blades. It wasn't too hot yet—mid-eighties that afternoon—and the air had a silky feel against her skin. A cheeky squirrel squawked at her from a tree branch, and she paused to grin up at it.

She was just mounting the front steps when the door swung back and there was Granny Dusty stand-ing behind the storm door in Wranglers and rawhide boots and a tight plaid Western shirt. She shoved open the storm door, too. "Wait till I tell you. Baby doll, you are not going to believe this."

Tate, Molly thought, her stomach knotting and the tension yanking tight between her shoulders again. Oh, God, what had he done? Had he been there, had he had it out with Granny?

Granny Dusty had a reputation, pretty much deserved, as the man-hatingest woman in Throckleford County. She had trusted one man in her life—the wrong one. A rich rancher from Montana, he'd come to town to do business with the Tates. The rancher knocked up Dusty with Molly's mother, Dixie, and then promptly went back to his wife on his big spread outside of Bozeman. After the rancher from Montana, Dusty O'Dare had no more use for men.

"What happened?" Molly asked weakly.

"That fool mother of yours says she's marrying Ray, that's what."

Not about Tate. Molly's stomach unknotted and her heart stopped trying to break out of her rib cage.

Granny continued with bitter relish, "She called here an hour ago, that mother of yours, all atwitter with the news. I ask you, sweetness, has she lost what is left of her mind? Ray Deekins is a no-count. He hasn't had a job since the Reagan years. And your mother is forty-six. You'd think she'd have grown out of all this love foolishness by now. Isn't it enough that she's let him move in with her? Can't she just support his lazy butt and leave it at that? Does she have to go and get herself legally *committed* to him? What is the matter with—?"

"Granny."

Granny glared—but at least she stopped talking.

"You think maybe I could get in the house before you start in about Ray?"

Granny Dusty smiled then, the network of wrinkles in her leathery cheeks scoring all the deeper. "Why sure, sugar, you just come on in." She held the storm door wider. Molly mounted the steps and entered the house. Beyond the door, the savory smell of fried meat filled the air. "Made your favorite," said Granny. "Chicken-fried steak."

Though as a rule Molly loved a good chicken-fried steak as much as the next person, that night her stomach clenched tight again at the thought. "Maybe later. I have a sick headache. Think I'd better lie down."

Now Granny got worried. "Honey pie, you got a fever? Want me to—"

"No. Really. Just a little rest, that'll do me fine." Molly headed for the house's one tiny hallway and her bedroom, the front one that faced the walk.

Granny followed right after her, causing Molly to have to remind herself that most of the time, she actually enjoyed having her grandmother living in her house. "I'll keep your supper warm for you," Granny said fondly as Molly sank to the edge of the bed and slipped off her sandals.

"Great." She forced a wan smile and flopped back onto the pillows, stretching her legs out and settling in, letting her eyes drift shut. "Thanks…"

"Maybe a cool cloth for your poor, tired eyes?" suggested Granny.

Molly's smile widened and she let out a soft chuckle. "What are you, a mind reader?"

"Be back in a flash."

Molly heard the water running and a minute later

her grandmother's capable hands smoothed a lovely cool washcloth over her eyes. "Um. Perfect..."

"Oh," Granny said. "Almost forgot. That Tate Bravo called. Told him you weren't in. Said I'd give you the message, but he shouldn't hold his breath waitin' for you to call back."

Molly lay very still with the cloth hiding her eyes as Granny cackled in satisfaction at having put the rich and powerful Tate Bravo in his place. Granny reveled in the council-meeting wrangling that went on between Molly and Tate. She loved to go on about all the ways Molly had bested "that Tate." She thought her granddaughter's dealings with Tate were strictly about politics and the betterment of the town. As of yet Molly had failed to bring her granny up to speed on the rolling-around-in-bed, ending-up-pregnant part of her and Tate's relationship.

"Thanks, Granny," Molly whispered, turning her head toward the wall. At least, she thought, he'd left her alone at the shop.

"Rest now," said Granny softly. A moment later, Molly heard the door click shut behind her.

Tate had called.

Unbidden, Molly felt the all-too-familiar tug of longing. It was awful. She wanted him so much— despite knowing that he was the absolute worst person in the world for her.

She let out a long sigh. She would *have* to call him back.

Eventually.

But not right now. Now, she was taking slow, even breaths. She was commanding her headache to pass and her stomach to stop churning. For the time being, she was resting right here in the peace of her own bedroom and she wasn't going to think about Tate Bravo or the baby or any of that.

For a half hour or so, Molly lay there on her bed, repeating soothing words in her head, breathing in and out slowly and deeply. She hovered on the verge of dropping off to sleep at last when she heard the front door open.

"Hey. Get along. Now. Go on," Granny called from out on the porch. There was a moment of silence and then, "Get the hell away from here, now. I have warned you and I will not be warning you again."

A man's voice answered from down the walk— Tate's? Molly wasn't sure. Whoever he was, she couldn't make out his words. She removed the wet cloth from over her eyes and set it on the nightstand.

"You remember, I warned you," said Granny. Molly sat up.

"Listen here, now," the man argued. "Put that thing down."

Molly groaned. It was Tate, all right. He was closer to the house, coming up the driveway. She swung her feet to the floor.

Granny said, "Not another damn step."

Tate said, "I'm not leaving till I talk to—" A thunderous blast cut him off.

Granny must have fired her shotgun at him.

Chapter Three

Molly flew off the bed, flung back the bedroom door, took the hall in a step and a half and shot across the small living room in four big strides. The front door stood open. Through the storm door, she could see her granny, who was muttering to herself and chambering another round. Molly shoved open the storm door. "Granny. Don't you put another round in that thing."

"Tell this crazy woman to put that gun down," Tate shouted from behind the big oak by the front walk.

Granny, who had the gun broken open and the barrel pointed at the porch boards for the moment, grumbled loudly, "Now look what you did. You went and woke her up."

"What is going on out here?" Molly cried.

''Gettin' rid of a little oversized vermin, sweetie pie, that's all.''

Molly's headache was back, with a vengeance. She shut the storm door and rubbed her forehead. ''Give me that shotgun.''

Granny flattened her lips. ''No need to get your drawers in a twist. It was only a warning shot, and I aimed good and high. Cleared his big, fat head by a mile. Not a scratch on him, I guarantee it.''

Molly quit rubbing her forehead and stuck out her hand, wiggling the fingers in a commanding way. ''Give it here.'' Granny mumbled something rude, but she did lock the barrel without shoving in a shell. ''Now,'' Molly commanded. Grudgingly Granny handed over the gun. ''Now go on inside this instant.'' Molly allowed no weakness in her voice. Sometimes, with Granny, you had to be really tough. ''Get in there and let me have a minute to talk to Tate.''

''What could you possibly have to say to the likes of him, honey bun?''

''I mean it, Granny.''

''But there's no reason you should have to—''

''Inside.'' Molly looked at her grandmother dead on, no blinking. After maybe ten seconds of that, Granny gave in. Grumbling under her breath in obvious disapproval, she banged through the storm door. Molly waited till she disappeared from view before calling to Tate, ''You can come out now.''

Dark eyes narrowed and broad shoulders straight, Tate emerged from behind the tree and mounted the porch steps. ''What is *wrong* with that woman?''

Molly ignored the way watching him come toward

her made her palms go sweaty and her heart beat faster. She gave him her coolest look. "Nothing the total elimination of the male sex from the world wouldn't cure."

For that, she got a slow once-over, starting at the top of her head and ending at her bare toes. "Having a little nap?"

She resisted the pitiful urge to fluff her pillow-flattened hair. "What's it to you?"

"It's good that you get your rest, that's all. You need it, for the baby's sake." It wasn't a bad thing to say, not really.

Still, another sour remark rose to her lips. She held it back.

He studied her for a long moment while she told herself that the hot shiver sliding through her meant nothing at all. Finally he said in a low, calm tone, "We need to talk, don't you think?"

She just felt so...defensive. It made her stiffen her spine and mutter provokingly, "As if you ever did care what *I* think."

He took a step closer. "Molly." The way he whispered her name made her yearn to throw her arms around him and beg him to take her right there on the front porch, to take her and never, ever let her go.

Hah. Never let her go. As if *that* would happen—as if she *wanted* it to happen.

She didn't. Uh-uh. No way. She did not...

"All right," she said, resigned to the fact that they were getting to the part with the shouting and the accusations. "We'll talk." She still had the shotgun in one hand. With the other, she gestured at the porch rocker. "Have a seat. I'll be right back." She whirled around and went inside before he could say another word.

"Granny?" she called softly. There was no answer. The only sound was the whir of the big window air conditioner in the kitchen.

Molly stepped over to the hallway. The door to the back bedroom was shut. Good. She went into her own room and straight to the closet, where she lifted a hidden trapdoor to a two-by-four-foot space under the floor. She put the shotgun in there and closed it up. She was reasonably certain Granny didn't know about that hiding space, which meant she wouldn't be threatening any unfortunate men with the shotgun for a while.

The weapon safely hidden away, Molly put on her sandals, grabbed her red purse and went to tap on Granny's door. "Tate and I have a few things to talk about. I'll be gone for a while."

The door opened. Granny looked at her sideways, graying brows drawn together. "You sure you know what you're doing?"

Molly forced a smile and leaned over to place a kiss on her weathered cheek. "I'll be back later."

"Where's my shotgun?"

"Safe."

"Humph," said Granny.

Molly leaned closer. "You can't go around shooting at men for no reason."

"Molly, baby, all men need shooting at. No reason required."

Molly shook her head. "You're lucky he isn't talking about suing you."

"Suing me? That's what's the matter with this

country nowadays. You fire a shot over a varmint's head and he takes you straight to court. And besides, what do I have that a rich man would sue for?''

''Granny, just settle down and behave, will you?''

Granny pinched up her mouth. ''You call me if he gives you too much grief. I'll see he regrets the day he ever messed with us O'Dares.''

Back out on the porch, Molly told Tate, ''We can't talk here. Granny's kind of fired up.'' No telling what she would do if Molly and Tate started trading hostile words. ''Let's go out to the Double T. We can talk in private there.''

''Good idea.'' He started to reach for her.

She stepped back. ''I'll take my own car.'' That way, when the yelling was over, she wouldn't be dependent on him for a ride home.

''Suit yourself.'' He turned without another word and went down the steps ahead of her.

The Double T ranch house stood, graceful and welcoming, at the end of a long curving driveway lined with oaks. The main—or center—wing had been built at the turn of the last century by Tate's great-great-grandfather, Tucker Tate II. The North Wing had been added by Tucker Tate III and the South Wing by Tate's grandfather, Tucker Tate IV. Since Tate was the only family member currently in residence, he lived in the main wing and left the other two to the occasional attentions of his housekeeper and the day maids.

He pulled his Cadillac into the central turnaround at the front of the house. Jesse Coutera, who drove him occasionally and acted as a general handyman around the place, was waiting for him. "Thanks, Jesse. Go ahead and put it away."

Molly's little red pickup screeched to a stop way too close to Tate's rear bumper. "And the lady's pickup?" Jesse asked, looking nervous, the way most men did around Molly. Molly, scowling, got out of the pickup and slammed the door.

"Better just leave it here for now," Tate said.

Jesse got in behind the wheel of the Caddy and headed down the side driveway. Molly approached. Though he'd already given her a good once-over back at her house, Tate couldn't help but do it again. She was dressed to match her pickup: red knee-length pants that clung to every generous curve, red sandals and a tight red T-shirt with Prime Cut in white lariat script across those breasts that no red-blooded male could keep from gaping at.

"Let's get this over with," she growled.

It was kind of depressing, how hostile she was. But he figured her attitude would change as soon as she got a look at the eight-carat diamond he'd driven to Abilene and bought her that afternoon.

Tate allowed himself a smug little smile. Since she'd climbed in his window the night before and dropped the bomb on him, Tate had been giving their little problem a lot of serious thought. He'd decided he was going to do the right thing and put a ring on Molly's finger.

"What are you grinning about?" She glowered at him, her big amber eyes narrowed to slits.

Uh-uh. She was not getting his dander up. "Shall we go inside?" He offered his arm.

She pointedly *didn't* take it. "Fine."

Tate led her to the big family room at the back of the center wing. The housekeeper, Miranda—Jesse's wife—appeared briefly to ask if there was anything she could get for them.

Molly shook her head tightly and tossed her shiny red bag on a chair. Tate thanked Miranda and told her he wouldn't need her again that night. She smiled and nodded and left them alone.

Molly was pacing, her heels clicking on the Spanish tiles of the floor every time she cleared one of the bright Navajo rugs.

"Sit down, why don't you?" Tate gestured at a tufted leather love seat as she stalked past it.

"Thanks. I'll stand." She stopped, wrapped her arms around herself, and faced him. "So, okay. Talk."

It wasn't exactly an inviting opening. But then, a man didn't get a lot of good openings with a prickly type like Molly.

She made a low, impatient sound and started pacing again. He watched her, admiring the sway of her full hips, aware that she was probably worried he would give her a hard time, maybe even try to tell her he didn't think the baby was his.

Tate had no doubt it was his. After all, she'd been a virgin the first time he made love to her—a damned eager virgin, but a virgin nonetheless.

He grinned every time he thought about that. Her virginity had shocked the hell out of him, if you want it straight. Molly was as sexy as they come and not the least bit shy. He'd just assumed she'd had her share of men.

But she hadn't. And she *was* honest. Crazy as she

made him sometimes, Tate knew her word was something he would never have cause to doubt. If she said she was having a baby and that baby was his, well, then he had to accept that he really was going to be a dad—which meant he was obligated to do the right thing and make her his bride.

Tate was feeling just fine about this particular obligation. He had a sense of a certain nobility within himself. He'd made the right decision; he would do the right thing.

Yeah, there would be talk. First, because everyone in town assumed that he and Molly hated each other, no one knew that they'd had an affair. Secondly, folks generally expected that when the time came for him to choose a bride, he would marry a woman from a socially prominent and well-to-do family.

Truth to tell, he'd had the same expectations himself. But he was thirty-four. And he'd yet to meet the paragon of womanhood who was supposed to make him want to settle down. And now there was Molly.

If before, Tate Bravo had shown little interest in finding himself a paragon, since Molly, his interest has dropped to flat zero.

So no problem. He would get by without the perfect wife. He would do his duty *and* have Molly in his bed from now on.

And there was another benefit beyond the great sex. Once Molly was his wife, he might get a little control over her when it came to running his town.

Molly stopped pacing again and braced her fists on the fine, womanly swell of her hips. "Well." She tapped her red toes. "Are you just going to stand there all night, gaping at me with that ridiculous, self-satisfied grin on your face?''

He felt his temper rise a little and ordered it down. ''Molly, Molly. There is absolutely no reason for you to be so damn mean to me.''

''Look. Can you just say it? Can you just go ahead and say it, please?''

Every word had an icicle hanging from it. But at least she'd said please.

Tate launched into the speech he'd been composing and rehearsing all day. ''Ahem. Molly. Since your, er, visit last night, I have been giving long and serious thought to what you said to me. I have looked at the situation from just about every angle, and no matter how I approach it, there seems to me to be only one solution.'' Tate paused.

He couldn't read Molly's expression. Struck dumb with shock? Moved beyond words? No way to tell. He crossed to the *pinero* wood mantel that his great-great-grandfather had ordered from Mexico and rested an elbow on it. Above the mantel hung one of his mother's paintings. Penelope Tate Bravo had studied art—to little effect that Tate could see—for a year at UCLA. It was there, in L.A., that she met Tate's father, the mysterious Blake Bravo. Tate pretended to admire the painting—of a poorly proportioned chestnut gelding and a stunted looking vaquero in a huge sombrero—as he gathered his thoughts to go on.

''Molly, there are many who will be shocked when they hear of our plans. And to that I say, so be it. I don't care in the least. They'll get used to it soon enough. The important thing is that you and I give our baby the right kind of start in life, that we put aside our differences and work together to ensure—''

"Tate…" Molly said his name hoarsely and then swallowed. With obvious difficulty.

He felt a tad irked with her for interrupting. "Can't you let a man say what he's trying to say?" In a minute would come the part where he got down on his knees in front of her. He was a little nervous about that. After all, he wasn't the kind of man who spent a lot of time on his knees.

"But, Tate…" She swallowed again. "I…I have to know. Are you, well, I mean, is it possible you are sneaking up on suggesting we get married?"

He smiled. How could he help it? She looked so damned adorable in her bewilderment. Also, it was occurring to him that he could skip the part where he got down on his knees. She'd pretty much blown right on by that, anyway.

Yeah. This was fine. It would work out just great. And with everything settled, she would be spending the night—and all the nights to come. "Yeah, Molly." Pride made him stand away from the mantel and draw himself up straight and tall. "I am. I'm asking you to be my wife. I figure, at this point, there's nothing else we can do." He reached into his pocket to get the ring.

Before he could slide it out, she said, "No."

Tate was certain he hadn't heard right. "Molly, did I just hear you say—?"

"No. I said no."

He pulled his hand from his pocket—without the ring—and took a careful step back. She'd got him on this one. Got him good. This was as unexpected as a rattler in his bedroll.

And damned if he wasn't as hurt as if he'd really been snake bit. Why, she hadn't even let him get to the part where he could flash that diamond at her. To cover his hurt, he gave her a curled lip and a cold eye.

She backed away a step herself and did some more gulping. "Look, Tate, it would never work. You have to see that. And why would you want to even try? Think of your granddaddy. Of what he'd say."

"My grandfather is dead. It doesn't matter what he'd say. Like I already told you, it doesn't matter a tinker's damn what anybody says. It's the right thing to do. And we are going to do it."

"No." She put up both hands, palms out, kind of warding him off. "No, Tate. We're not."

It took all the considerable will and self-restraint he possessed not to grab her and turn her over his knee. She could use a good paddling, oh, yes, she could. "Molly, darlin'." He kept his voice low—and deadly. "You have said a lot of stupid things since I have had the pleasure of knowing you. But saying no to me right now, that's a new high in stupidity. Even for you."

She fell back another step—but her eyes had that look in them—the look that said he'd better watch out. "Don't you call me stupid, you big macho butt-head."

Macho butt-head? He felt his blood pressure go up a notch and ordered it back down. "Molly, you have got to see—"

"I don't have to see squat. We are not getting married, Tate Bravo. What do either of us know about marriage? Not a damn thing. Well, except this. I do know this. When people get married, they ought to at least know how to get along with each other first. You and me? We never get along. We're either fighting or ripping each other's clothes off and racing for the bed. What kind of marriage would the likes of us have? I shudder to imagine, I truly do.''

By then, Tate's urge to yank her over his knee and paddle her good was so powerful it caused a pounding behind his eyes. With great effort, he clung to reasonable discourse—or at least, to a low, controlled tone. ''You are the future mother of my child, Molly. And by God, you are going to marry me.''

She marched over and snatched her purse off the chair. ''No, I am not.'' She was already headed for the front hall.

''Molly,'' he commanded. ''Molly, get back here.'' She didn't so much as break her stride. ''Molly. Damn you.'' He took off after her.

In the hallway, she turned on him. ''Stop, Tate. Stop right there.''

''Molly—''

''I'm going home now. Do you hear me? Home. Alone.''

''The hell you are. Why can't you be reasonable?''

''Reasonable?'' she scoffed. ''Now, that's one of those words, isn't it, Tate?''

''One of those words? What are you babbling about?''

''You know what words I'm talking about. The kind of words that mean *do things Tate's way*. There are a lot of words like that, in case you haven't noticed. Words like *right* and *good* and *logical* and *fair*. Around you, Tate, those words always mean one thing. They mean *your way*. Because your way is the right, good, logical and fair way. Isn't it?''

How, he wondered, could he want her so much when she was such a complete bitch? It was, and probably always would be, a mystery to Tate. ''Don't you walk out that door on me, Molly.''

''Oh. Oh, of course. Give me orders. *Dream* that I'm going to obey them.''

''I mean it. Don't leave.''

Molly gave him a long, hot look. And then she whirled, marched to the door and flung it open. She went through and slammed it behind her. It was a heavy, carved door. It had come up from Mexico with the mantel in the living room. It made a loud, echoing, *final* sort of sound when slammed.

Tate stood in the entry hall with his blood pounding in his ears and listened to her pickup rev high outside. Peeling rubber, she took off.

This is not the end of it, Molly, he silently promised her.

Whether she wanted to or not, it was reasonable, right, good, logical *and* fair that she marry him. And one way or another, Tate Bravo always did what was reasonable, right, good, logical and fair.

Chapter Four

Lena Lou Billingsworth stuck her hand out from under the red cutting cape and fluttered her thick eyelashes at Molly. "Molly, you didn't even ask to see it."

Molly took Lena's soft little hand. "Gorgeous," she declared. "Absolutely gorgeous."

Lena preened. "Four carats." Back in high school, Lena and Tate's wandering younger brother, Tucker, had been an item. But that was a decade ago. "Dirk is *so* generous." Lena's fiancé owned a couple of car dealerships on the outskirts of nearby Abilene. "You know, Molly, some say every girl is only lookin' for a man like her daddy. I believe that now, I truly do." Lena Lou's daddy, Heck Billingsworth, was a car dealer, too—a big, bluff fellow who never met a man he didn't like, let alone a vehicle he couldn't sell.

A man just like her daddy, huh? Finding such a man would be a big challenge for Molly, as she'd never met her daddy and wouldn't have recognized him if she bumped into him on the street.

At fifteen, Molly's mom, Dixie, had lost her virginity to a traveling salesman who discovered the next morning that the pretty young thing he'd seduced the night before was underage. On hearing the news, the salesman promptly threw his samples in the trunk of his Chrysler New Yorker and burned rubber getting the heck outta town.

Dixie never heard from the guy again—and nine months later, Molly arrived. So, truly, Molly never knew her father. In fact, she didn't even know his name. When Dixie asked for it that fateful night, the salesman replied in a lazy Southern drawl, ''You just call me Daddy, sugar-buns.''

Funny, Molly was thinking. She'd never known her dad—and her mom seemed more like a sweet and wild and often absent big sister to her than any real kind of mom. Mostly, in Molly's growing-up years, Dixie was busy with her active social life. Dixie would climb out the window as soon as Granny Dusty went to bed and wiggle back in around dawn, half-drunk, with her mascara running down her cheeks and her clothes looking like she'd torn them off and rolled around on them—which, more than likely, she had. She would sleep until noon, then get up and eat cold cereal or maybe cream cheese on a cracker and wander around the double-wide trailer in a kind of good-natured daze until dark—at which time she would lock herself in the bathroom to shower, fix her hair and do her makeup. As soon as Granny went to bed, she would climb out the window all over again.

Dixie O'Dare had always been a woman on a mission to find the man who would love her forever and treat her right. She never had a lot of luck in her quest. And since it consumed most of her time and energy, Granny Dusty had ended up taking care of Molly.

Molly wanted things to be different for *her* baby. She was going into this all grown up with her eyes wide open. She wouldn't be wasting her energy chasing after men. She would take her child-rearing seriously. And her baby girl—Molly just knew her baby had to be a girl—would at least know who her father was, even if Molly did not intend to marry the man.

Tate, Molly thought, shaking her head. She'd imagined him saying a lot of ugly things. But a marriage proposal? Not on your life.

And okay, maybe she'd been a little hard on him last night. Especially considering he'd put up with Granny shooting at him and he hadn't called Molly one single rude name. But she was not going to marry him, and he had to accept that.

Sadly, Tate was one of those men who never heard what a woman said unless she shouted it out good and loud. And even then, the chance was never better than fifty/fifty the words would get through that thick skull of his.

Lena was still talking. "The wedding will be next June—I know, I know. It's a whole year away. But a wedding is something a girl plans for her whole life. I want everything to be perfect. And it's always been my dream to be a June bride."

"A June bride," Molly parroted brightly. "That is just so romantic," she said and set about cutting and shaping Lena's thick auburn hair.

Lena said, "I'll have Lori Lee up from San Antonio to be my matron of honor. She hasn't been home in I don't know how long. But for this, for my wedding, you can bet she'll be here." Lori Lee was Lena's identical twin, though no one ever had any trouble telling them apart. Lena was the popular one, a real sparkler. Lori Lee was quieter, less flashy, more serious—or at least, she had been ten years ago when she graduated from high school and left town suddenly, rarely to return.

Molly nodded. "That all just sounds perfect..." Lena talked, and Molly finished up her cut and blew her dry.

The salon was packed today. Molly had three other stylists working, as well as a receptionist, a shampoo girl and a nail technician. Everyone was booked through closing—and still they had walk-ins filling the reception area, thumbing through the magazines, waiting their turn, everyone laughing and chatting away.

Some of them wouldn't get their hair done today. But the women didn't mind. Molly had all the current fashion and hairstyle magazines, comfortable chairs for them to sit in, and the coffee and cold tea were free. They talked town politics and shared the latest gossip. The Cut was the place every woman in town went when she wanted a few laughs, some serious girl talk and all the freshest, juiciest dirt on who was doing what with whom.

"Heard your mom is marrying Ray," said Donetta

Brewer. She sat in one of the soft red reception chairs, thumbing through a *Lucky* magazine, waiting her turn in Molly's styling chair. Donetta always seemed to know things no one else had heard yet. "Fourth of July," she added, "out in Emigration Park."

The date and the location were news to Molly. But she didn't let Donetta know it. "Yep. Looks like it."

"Ray is a sweet man," declared Emmie Lusk, ensconced in Molly's chair by then, getting her hair rolled for a perm. Like Donetta, Emmie kept an ear to the ground when it came to town tittle-tattle. "Good at heart, he truly is." Which meant that, while he didn't have a job, at least he didn't knock Dixie around the way most of her other boyfriends had. "I'm sure they'll both be very happy." Emmie met Molly's eyes in the mirror, and Emmie's large, thin-lipped mouth stretched into the widest, most saccharine of smiles.

Molly, accustomed to talk about Dixie and her boyfriends, smiled calmly in return and went on rolling Emmie's expertly tinted sable-brown hair. "Make an appointment for some color, Emmie, before you leave today. These roots are starting to show."

After Dixie and Ray's upcoming nuptials, the talk moved on to Lena and Dirk. "A whole year till the wedding. What is *that* about?" Emmie wondered aloud.

Donetta said, "A big wedding takes time. You know that. But did you hear her? A sit-down prime rib dinner for two hundred. Good old Heck had better sell a lot of cars."

"And didn't she say Lori Lee will have to come?" asked another customer.

"Hah," said Donetta. "Can't wait to see that—and that little boy of hers, too. Nine years old. And she was married for six. Just widowed, did you hear? Met her husband in San Antonio three years after that kid was born. I heard that when she found out she was pregnant, she wouldn't tell who the father was. Heck yelled and threatened and snapped his belt around, but Lori Lee refused to say. The minute she finished her senior year, Heck packed her up and sent her to San Antonio. I'll sure be intrigued to see who that little boy resembles."

"She hardly dated," said Emmie. "Always the quiet one. I'd guess the father is no one we know. More than likely some stranger who blew into town and then blew right back out again. We all know that does happen." Emmie sent Molly an arch kind of look. After all, that was just what had happened to Dixie, now wasn't it—with Molly the result?

Molly gave Emmie her very blandest smile and then tuned out the avid speculation as to the missing daddy of Lori Lee's love child. She also tried not to think about the things Donetta and Emmie would be saying as soon as the word got out that Molly was having Tate Bravo's baby.

It was not going to be pretty. But she figured she had at least a month or two—maybe even longer if she watched what she ate—before she started to show and the tongues started wagging. Molly was determined to fully enjoy the time left before scandal engulfed her.

Molly rolled up Emmie's hair quickly and had just donned her plastic gloves to sponge on the solution when the bell over the door tinkled and Donetta, who'd been talking nonstop for fifteen minutes, suddenly shut up. As a matter of fact, the whole shop went pin-drop quiet. Molly glanced toward the door.

Tate.

Oh, please, God, she thought, not here. Not now…

"May I help you?" asked Molly's receptionist Darlene, hopefully.

Tate barreled right on past Darlene and went straight to where Molly stood. He made a sick face at the smell of the solution and then announced, "Molly. I'd like a word with you. Now."

Behind her *Lucky* magazine, Donetta gasped. In the mirror, Emmie's eyes were wide and bulging, like a Pekinese just prior to a barking fit.

Calm, Molly silently commanded herself. *Stay calm. Don't let him get to you.* "Well, as you can see, I am busy right now."

"Get unbusy."

She tried a little noble outrage. "I cannot believe you have the gall to march right into my place of business and start giving me orders, Tate Bravo."

He grunted. "Yeah, so? I'm big in the gall department and you know it, too. You damn well should have figured this would happen last night when you walked out on me."

Donetta and Emmie gasped in unison that time.

In the mirror, Molly saw that her face had flushed the same color as the walls and the reception chairs. She could have scratched out his eyes on the spot for that, for making her blush deep red in her own place of business. She opened her mouth to order him out and then shut it before she spoke. She could see by the granite set to his square jaw that demanding he leave would be an exercise in futility. He would still be here and she would look more ineffectual that she looked already.

So what, then? Call the chief of Tate's Junction's two-man police department? Yeah, right. Everyone knew Police Chief Ed Polk was in Tate Bravo's pocket—just like most of the other officials in town.

"I'm sorry," Molly said, tone sweet as honey, teeth clenched tight. "I can't talk right now. I have to finish this perm. And after that, I have four cut-and-blow-dries and three weaves to do."

"Take a break."

"I will not."

Tate grabbed for the bowl of solution. Molly snatched it away, almost spilling it down the back of Emmie's neck. Emmie let out a cry of distress.

"Look." Molly set the bowl down, stepped right up to Tate and lifted her face so they were nose to nose. "You are scaring my customers. Kindly get the hell out of my shop."

He stepped back, stood straight to his full six foot three and folded those big, hard arms across his wide chest. "Not until we have a talk."

"We *have* talked," she reminded him in a tone so low he probably wouldn't have heard it if everyone else in the shop hadn't been holding their breaths and sitting absolutely still, staring with wide, eager eyes.

"We sure as hell haven't talked enough."

"It doesn't matter how much we talk," she told him. "Nothing is going to change."

"We'll see about that." He glanced around. "You got an office in this place where we can have a little privacy?"

A thought came to her. She would stall him. Maybe if she stalled long enough, he would give up and go away. She tugged neatly—for emphasis—on her latex gloves and then picked up her bowl of solution again. "I can't speak to you right this minute. A perm simply can't wait. Have a seat in the reception area— enjoy a cup of coffee or some cold tea if you'd like. I'll be with you as soon as I can."

He looked at her sideways, those fine, sculpted lips curling in obvious suspicion. "Molly." He muttered her name, making a warning of it.

"I'm sorry, Tate. You'll just have to wait." She pointed at the one free chair—right next to Donetta. "Go on. Sit over there."

It worked. He wasn't happy about it, but he strode over to that chair and dropped into it.

Donetta kind of craned back away from him, gulped and tried weakly, "Well, hi there, Tate. How've you been?"

"Hello, Donetta," he growled. He picked up a magazine, looked at the cover of it and tossed it right back down.

"How is that brother of yours?" asked Donetta. "I haven't seen him in years. He's been missing longer than the Bravo Baby, and that's a fact." She was grinning by then, as if she'd said something really clever.

Tate didn't seem to see the humor. The Bravo Baby—no relation to Tate or his brother—had been kidnapped years and years ago. Coast to coast, everyone knew the story of how he'd vanished from his crib in his wealthy parents' Bel Air mansion. A huge ransom had been paid, but the baby was never returned. He'd been found, a grown man, alive and well, a few years back, after going missing for three decades.

Tucker hadn't been gone nearly that long.

Tate, however, had sense enough not to point that out. He probably knew it would only encourage Donetta. Instead he replied stiffly, "It's been a while since I've seen Tucker, myself."

Donetta tried again to get a little more information out of him. "Loves to travel, doesn't he?" she asked brightly. "I hear he's been all over the world."

Tate looked at her, dead on. "That's right," he said. The set of his shoulders and the icy look in his eyes clearly indicated that the conversation was concluded.

Donetta took the hint. She raised her magazine and pretended to read it with all her might.

Tate gave up looking for reading material. He sat in the red chair and stared straight ahead. For a while, the Cut was way too quiet. In time, though, the women did begin talking again—but furtive and soft, the way people whisper at funerals or in church.

Molly finished putting the solution on Emmie, set the timer and moved her to another chair. She took off her plastic gloves. "Donetta, let's have Charlee get you shampooed."

Donetta eagerly put down her magazine and headed for the sinks where Charlee, the shampoo girl, would take good care of her.

Tate stood. The place went dead silent again.

Molly shook her head. "Sorry. No can do right yet." She beamed him a big, fake smile.

Tate glared—but he did sit back down. Molly went

over and made a show of checking on Emmie, though really there was nothing to check on as yet. Then, since it would be a few minutes until Charlee was done with Donetta, Molly headed for the back door. Out in the alley, she crouched behind the big shop Dumpster and waited for enough time to pass that she could start on Donetta.

Five minutes later, she reentered the shop. Tate was right there waiting by the door. "Where did you get off to?" he demanded.

She edged around him. "Excuse me. I'm working, here."

Charlee had already led Donetta to the chair and put the cape on her. Molly set to work on Donetta's hair. Tate, who had followed behind her from the back door, hovered a few feet away, looking dangerous. But after a few minutes of that, he gave up and went back to sit down.

Molly cut and blew Donetta dry. By then, Emmie was ready for the setting solution and the rinse. Molly put her gloves back on and took care of it. Then Emmie had to be dried and combed out.

By the time she whipped the cape off of Emmie— about an hour and a quarter after Tate had first entered the shop—he was getting pretty edgy. Molly kept sending him careful sideways glances.

Uh-uh. Not good. He wasn't giving up and going away as she'd secretly hoped he might—and he wasn't sitting still for this waiting game much longer.

Just as she'd expected, two or three minutes later, he stood. "Molly, I've had it. Either you talk to me in private—now—or we will have our little conversation right here with all these lovely, *interested* ladies listening in.''

Molly looked in his eyes and knew she couldn't stall him another minute longer. So all right, she thought. She would take him into her office and tell him all over again what she'd told him last night.

How many times was she going to have to tell him? Judging by his mulish expression, too many.

Or maybe he actually had something new to say. It could happen. After all, anything was possible.

''Emmie, you can settle up with Darlene and she'll get you scheduled for that color—next week?''

Emmie nodded and moved to the reception desk. The place had gone deathly quiet again. And though Donetta had already had her cut, she hadn't left. Oh, no. She'd plunked herself right back down in that red chair and picked up the same magazine she'd already read at least twice.

A feeling of equal parts bottomless dread and glum resignation dragged on Molly. Those two scandal-free months she'd been anticipating were starting to look more and more unlikely.

She turned to Leslie Swankstad, her next customer. ''Sorry, Leslie. I'll be a few minutes.''

''Oh, no problem,'' Leslie said, sounding breathless. ''No problem at all.''

''This way,'' Molly told Tate and turned for the hall at the back of the shop.

She led him through the last door on the right before the exit door at the end. Inside she had her desk and computer, a couple of four-drawer file cabinets, some display shelves with various hair-care products on them and two red plastic guest chairs. She signaled

Tate toward the guest chairs and shut the door, closing them into the small space together, instantly feeling that there wasn't enough room.

In an effort to get as far away from him as possible,
she went around behind the desk and dropped into
her swivel chair. "All right. What?"

"You know what. Marry me."

Oh, wonderful. Of course. More of the same.
"Tate. We've been through this."

"Marry me."

Just great, she thought. He had one tune on this
subject and by golly, he was going to play it until he
drove her out of her mind. "Listen. Please." She really was trying to be gentle, to be reasonable. "Be
realistic."

"I am. You're having my baby. The way I see it,
that means you and me are getting married."

"No, Tate. We're not."

"Oh, yeah, we are."

Calm, she thought. *Stay calm. Be reasonable.* "I
want you to just think this over a little. Think about
how poorly suited we are to each other, how marriage
could never work for us. Tate, I'm an independent
woman from the wrong side of town and you're a
domineering rich man raised to think you own the
world."

He looked at her from under the heavy ridge of his
brow, his lip curled in a sneer. "So now you're insulting me…"

Molly sighed deeply and shook her head. She
leaned back in her chair. "No. I promise you. I'm not
trying to insult you. I'm just trying to make you see."

"What's there to see? You're pregnant and it's my kid and we need to get married immediately."

"Tate. We're a match made by the devil himself. You used to know that."

"Everything's different now. There's a baby on the way."

"No. No, really, nothing is different. Nothing has changed. You're still you and I'm still me and for us to get married would be a disaster. The baby would only suffer for it if we did."

Tate stood. He didn't look encouraging. He looked…about to start shouting. "I know what's right, and damn it, right is what I intend to do."

Molly stared up at him in despair. *So much for my month or two, scandal-free,* she thought. "Oh, Tate…"

"Molly," he said way too loudly, "you are going to marry me."

"No, I am not," she replied, her voice soft and low and steady as a rock. She stood. They confronted each other across her desk. "And I want you to leave now."

"You're not keeping this a secret," he said. "Don't think that you will. This isn't going to be like it was when we started in together, something only you and me will know about. And you can't end this the way you did when you dumped me, moaning about how you're tired of sneaking around and lying to the people who trust you. You are having my baby and by God, I'll shout it to the rooftops."

It was a challenge. What could she do but accept it? She felt a deep sadness then—for him. For herself. For the innocent baby who would have *them* for parents. Were there ever two people in the world so poorly suited to the state of matrimony? She didn't think so. And why couldn't he see that? Why did he have to be the kind of man who got something in his head and wouldn't let go of it?

"No way I *can* hide it in the end, Tate," she told him flatly. "So you go ahead. You shout it as loud as you want to. It won't change a thing. I'm not marrying you."

"Oh, but you will."

"Oh, no, I won't."

Calmly, he went over and opened the door. Out in the shop, it was quiet—very, very quiet. Molly could just picture them all out there—Donetta and Emmie and the rest of them—straining their ears in hopes of hearing just a few words of what was going on in Molly's office.

Tate made sure they got an earful. "Molly," he said, aiming the words out the door and speaking loudly enough to be heard all the way out past the shop's front door and onto Center Street, "you are having my baby and by God, if it's the last thing I do, I will see to it that you marry me."

He turned and looked at Molly, square chin up, hard jaw set. She said nothing. Really, Tate had pretty much said it all.

Out in the salon, it was so quiet, if she hadn't known better, Molly would have guessed that everyone had left.

Tate said, his voice soft now, but thick with suppressed anger, "Satisfied?"

"Get out of my shop," she replied, her tone every

bit as soft and full of fury as his. ''And do me a big favor. Never come back.''

With a final curt nod, Tate turned and went out—and not through the back door either, which was two feet from her office door and would have been the quickest way.

Oh, no. Not Tate Bravo. He marched right through the shop and out the front door. She heard the bell tinkle when he pulled the door open. ''Afternoon, ladies,'' he said.

The bell jingled cheerily again as the door shut behind him.

Chapter Five

By the next morning, the news was all over town.

Tate Bravo had gotten Molly O'Dare pregnant. He wanted to marry her. And she was having none of it.

The men shook their heads. The women took sides. All through the breakfast shift at Jim-Denny's Diner on Center Street, where Dixie had been waiting tables for fifteen years, there was lively debate.

"What is her problem?" Lena Lou, who'd dropped in for her usual decaf and English muffin, wanted to know. "Tate Bravo is studly and rich as they come." Lena paused to admire the way her engagement diamond glittered in the glare from the overhead florescent lights. Then she got back on topic. "When's Molly O'Dare gonna do better? She should snap that man up while she's got the chance."

"Oh, never," argued Emmie Lusk, fluffing her new

perm. "Never in this life. Our Molly has guts and gumption. She's not marrying anyone just 'cause she's pregnant. So what if he's handsome and rolling in dough? There's more to life than money, a good-looking husband and legitimate children, after all."

"Well, now, Emmie," Donetta said, "don't go discounting a fat bank account. It is a proven fact that the older a woman gets, the more she needs a rich husband—or at the very least, a viable retirement plan."

"If she marries him, what about her position as mayor of our town?" demanded Rosie Potts, whose mother was a shut-in and likely to benefit greatly from some of Molly's programs. "You know he'll corrupt her. Just see if he doesn't. I'm inclined to wonder if he hasn't already. Y'all have to admit, it's a shock. In bed with the enemy, that's where she's been."

"More coffee?" asked Dixie, pot poised over Donetta's cup. Donetta nodded and Dixie poured.

"Dixie," said Rosie. "She's your daughter. What do you think?"

Dixie smiled her secret smile at Ray, who sat sipping coffee in his favorite spot at the end of the counter. Ray gave her a wink. "Molly said she wouldn't marry him, didn't she?"

"Well, yeah, so?" Lena rattled her own cup.

Dixie filled it. "If Molly says she's not marrying him, then it doesn't matter a bit what Tate Bravo does or anybody says. She won't be marrying him. It's as simple as that."

"But that is plain stupid," Lena declared, rising and laying her money on the counter. "Why have a baby without a husband if you don't have to?" Lena

bit her pretty lip. Everyone knew she had to be thinking about her twin sister, Lori Lee. But then she covered her own discomfort with, ''No offense, Dixie.''

Dixie's beatific smile only widened. ''None taken.
And it just may be that I, personally, agree with you.
But like I said, what I think or you think isn't what
matters. It's Molly's decision and so far anyway, she
has said no.''

Molly had just climbed into bed and turned out the
light when the tap came at the window that faced the
front walk. Her first thought was *Tate,* and she
scowled into the darkness. If he kept this up, she
would be looking into getting a restraining order on
him. Just because he thought he had to marry her
wasn't any excuse for the man to turn stalker.

But then there was another tap—as soft and cautious as the first.

Hmm. Soft and cautious. Not Tate's style. More
like…

Molly slid from her bed and went to pull back the
curtain. Dixie stood on the other side, smiling. She
held up a brown bag with the neck of a liquor bottle
sticking out of it and smiled wider.

Molly pushed up the window. ''You know, you
could have just—'' Dixie cut her short by putting a
finger to her lips. Molly finished in a whisper,
''—come to the door.''

Dixie shook her big platinum-blond head of hair
and whispered back, ''Hon, I don't need to hear your
granny go on about my sweet Ray-boy and me getting
married. She wears me out, and I'm just not up for it
tonight, you know?'' She waved the bottle some

more, causing her chunky charm bracelet—silver balls dripping with pink plastic hearts—to rattle in a cheerful kind of way. The scent of White Diamonds, Dixie's favorite perfume, wafted in through the screen. "Can I come in?"

"What's in the bottle?"

"Jack Black, baby girl—and I don't mean the movie star."

"Didn't you hear? I'm pregnant."

Dixie made a big show of rolling her eyes. "Oh, I heard. All day long, I heard."

Though Molly had never been much of a drinker, getting blotto right then did hold some appeal. But no. She had to think of the baby. "No liquor for me."

"Well, that's fine." Dixie leaned a little closer to the screen. "I pretty much figured you'd say that. But you know how *I* am. Never had a problem with being the only one drinkin'."

Molly unhitched the screen and held it up. Dixie handed Molly the bottle and swung a leg over the sill, and Molly thought fondly about all the times she'd watched her mother climb through the window in the middle of the night.

Once she'd slithered inside, Dixie straightened her short, tight skirt, tugged on her tank top and then held out her hand. Molly gave her back her bottle. Dixie grabbed it by the neck, still in the bag. She screwed off the top and took a swig. Scrunching up her face tight, she swallowed. "Ungh!" she exclaimed, pounding her chest with a fist. "Ooo-wa!" And then she put her hand over her mouth and giggled. "Oops. Too loud," she whispered. "Mustn't forget your granny."

"Good thinking," Molly said dryly.

"Jack Black," Dixie murmured contentedly as she recapped the bottle, "really hits the spot." Bracelet rattling, she grabbed Molly's hand. "Come on. Let's sit." They both perched on the edge of the bed. "So, now. How're you holding up?"

"I'm getting by."

Dixie smoothed Molly's hair and gently cupped her chin. "You look kinda tired, baby."

"Yeah. Guess I am. It's all starting to get to me. Endless advice from any and everyone who comes in the shop. And some of the women in town are disappointed in me for sleeping with Tate in the first place, when he's the main one standing in the way of all the good things I want to do as mayor. Those women have let me know, in no uncertain terms, that they consider my having had sex with Tate to be nothing short of a betrayal of all I'm supposed to be standing for."

"Oh, pooh on them. They are just jealous. Tate Bravo is untamed and all man. Just let him crook a finger at any one of them. You'd better believe the chosen one would be naked and flat on her back faster than chain lightning with a link snapped." Dixie snapped her fingers high and sharp, just to show how fast that might be.

"Tate." Molly was shaking her head. "He's most of my problem. He keeps popping up out of nowhere to order me to marry him. He didn't show up today, but he might as well have. I stayed on edge every minute just worrying he might."

"So you're saying you don't—" Dixie paused to take another belt from her bottle, screw up her face and swallow "—want to marry him, right?" Molly looked away. "Well, do you or don't you?"

"It would never work."

Dixie took her face and guided it back around. Molly pushed her hand away. Dixie sighed. "You planning on answering my question? Sometime soon would be nice."

"I can't answer it."

"Because...?"

"Since it's not gonna work, it doesn't matter what I want."

Dixie looked kind of thoughtful. "So," she said, and paused for yet another big gulp. "You do care for him, then. Am I right?"

Molly hung her head and nodded.

Dixie's whisper got softer. "But the way he's been acting, he's not reassuring you that he would make a decent husband?"

Molly shrugged. "I guess. And then there's me. You know how I am. I do like to run things. And I have no idea at all about how to try to be a wife."

"Well, baby, some things you just do, you know? You learn as you go."

Molly looked straight at her mother. "It isn't going to work. Let's talk about something else, okay?"

Dixie giggled—but softly, ever-mindful that Granny shouldn't know she was there. She leaned close to Molly and whispered in her ear. "I know! I've been meaning to ask you. Be my maid of honor?"

Molly grunted out a scoffing sound and put her hand on her stomach. "Some *maid*."

Dixie grabbed her hand and kissed it. "Oh, silly girl. Who's a virgin at thirty, anyway?"

"I was…for a month or so."

Dixie let go of Molly's hand—and then wrapped her arm around Molly's shoulders. She gave a squeeze. "Say you will."

Molly looked up at her mother, smelling White Diamonds again—and the heady scent of Tennessee whiskey, as well. "You know I will."

"That's my baby." Dixie gave Molly's shoulder another squeeze. "And I might not have been much use to you while you were growing up, but maybe I can help now. I think I will have a little talk with that man of yours."

Molly pulled out of her mother's embrace. "He's not my man—and you better not."

"Is that a 'please don't'?"

"It's a 'why waste your breath!'"

Pink plastic hearts clattered together as Dixie raised her bottle of Jack Black high. "Baby, give your mama just a little bit of credit."

It was after eleven at night when the doorbell rang. Tate was in his study going over some of the accounts. Miranda had long since retired to the apartment over the garages that she shared with Jesse.

So Tate got up, turned off the alarm and answered the door himself. It was Molly's mother, Dixie O'Dare.

"Tate Bravo, I was wondering if I might have a word with you."

Since his study was right off the entry, he ushered

her in there. "Sit down." He gestured to the sitting area.

"Thank you." Dixie smiled that pretty smile of hers, but didn't move beyond the doorway. In her mid-forties, she was still a woman who turned heads. She had that fine, sweet smile and the kind of figure that got men thinking things they shouldn't. "Thank you," she said. "But I think I'll stand."

Tate went over to the liquor cart in the corner. "Drink?"

Molly's mother licked her full pink lips. She had a woozy look. Tate guessed she'd already had a few. "Better not," she said. "But thank you."

"Well, then. What can I do for you…?" Uncertain about how to address her, he let the question trail off.

"Dixie," she helpfully provided. "You just go ahead and call me Dixie."

"Dixie," he repeated, returning her smile, wishing that Molly could be half as agreeable as her mother.

"So, Tate…"

"Yeah?"

"I heard you want to marry my Molly."

He went around and dropped into his studded leather swivel chair. "That's right. Molly's having my child, and I'm going to marry her."

"Molly says you're not."

He sat forward. "Molly is wrong."

"See?" said Dixie. "See there, that's your problem. You're a man used to giving orders and having everyone say yes, sir. Right away, sir. Now, with a lot of women, that kind of he-man approach will work just fine. A lot of women go all weak in the knees when a real man starts bossing them around. But in case maybe you didn't notice, Molly's not like a lot of women.''

Good-looking as Dixie was, she was starting to get on his nerves. "Your point?''

"Well, maybe you could try cozying up to her a little.''

He grunted. "Since she's not letting me near her, cozying up is not looking real likely.''

"Well, and see? That's just what I meant. How you gonna marry my baby if she won't let you near her?''

It was a problem. He realized that. "So?'' he demanded gruffly.

"So, maybe you oughtta start by making sure you'll be welcome when you come calling at her house.''

He thought of Molly's grandmother—on the porch with the shotgun. "I could get killed trying that.''

Dixie giggled. "Well, Tate. That's why I'm here. I aim to help you out.''

He regarded her with frank suspicion. "How do you plan to do that?''

"You know that expression, 'salt the old cow to get to the calf'?''

"Dixie, you're hardly an old cow.''

Dixie glowed with pleasure at the compliment. "Why, thank you, Tate. But I wasn't referring to myself.''

Tate understood then. He made a sour face. "Dusty? You want me to suck up to Dusty?''

"*Sucking up* isn't exactly what I would have called it.''

"But it *is* what you meant.''

"Oh, now, Tate. It's not going to kill you.''

"Sucking up? Maybe not. But that crazy mother of yours just might."

"You only need to know *how* to make up to her. You need to know her likes and dislikes. Her secret yearnings…"

"Dusty O'Dare has got secret yearnings?" The idea kind of scared him.

"My mother's tough as a roll of barbed wire, but she is still a woman in her heart."

"Oh, yeah?" Could have fooled Tate.

"Now, Tate. That there's a big part of your problem. You need to get yourself in courting mode. And courting mode means you are always polite and respectful when referring to or addressing your darlin' one or any member of her family."

Tate wasn't sure he liked the idea of sucking up to Dusty. But he *was* getting the picture. "And that's why you're here? To help me make nice?"

Dixie got a kind of wistful look. "I could never have another child after Molly. It was a tough birth and…well, as a result, she is my one and only. I have been somewhat…distracted, when it came to being a mother. But like all mothers, I do want to see my only child happy, with a good man who'll love her till she pleads for mercy and provide her with a platinum no-limit credit card. I think you just might be that man. And I do believe that deep in her heart, Molly would prefer to be married to her baby's daddy. You say you want that, too."

"I do want that, Dixie," Tate said quietly.

The sad look vanished as Dixie smiled her dazzling smile. "Then grab a pen and a full-size piece of paper. This will be a long list…."

* * *

The next day, which just happened to be Friday the thirteenth, Molly got a lot more advice at work—and couple of expressions of deep disappointment that she'd gone and crawled into bed with Tate Bravo, of all people.

And like the day before, she kept waiting for Tate to come barreling through the door, demanding that she marry him on the spot. Also like the day before, he never appeared. Maybe, she thought philosophically, as time went by and he didn't come busting through the door, she would learn to relax a little again—if her customers would ever shut the heck up about him.

"Molly, love, you know you really owe it to your baby to let Tate do right by you, don't you think? You have to see he's only trying to do what's best. And once you're married to him, well, you won't have to work a lick if you're not of a mind to. You can stay home with your baby. Now, won't that be nice? And you're not that old, really. You might even be able to have two or three more."

"Molly, you hold firm, honey. Don't let him railroad you. Remember his poor mama, Penelope? Slinkin' around, scared of her own shadow? That's what comes of being raised and run by a Tate. And those awful paintings of hers... And then, how she died..." Penelope Tate Bravo had been broadsided by a semitruck while trying to pull out of the local ice-cream shop parking lot, after stopping in to get herself a double dip after church. "So very sad. And Tucker? Where did he come from? Now, think about that. Wasn't that mysterious husband of Penelope's supposed to have been long dead when Tucker came along? Not that I blame the poor woman, I tell you. If Tucker Tate the fourth was my daddy, I'd probably run off and get me something going with a stranger now and then, too. It was a pitiful life poor Penelope had. Don't let yourself or your baby fall into that trap...."

"Molly, Molly. I have to say it. You really have let us down, and I think you know it. I hope Tate Bravo has no hold on you other than the obvious one of having fathered your child. I hope when the next town council meeting comes, you're not turning wishy-washy when it comes to the programs we have all been counting on you to put through."

Listening to everyone go on and on wasn't easy. Molly feared she was reaching the boiling point, that the day would come—and soon—when she would yell at them all to shut up with their criticisms and endless advice, or get the hell out of her salon.

It would be bad for business to do that—not to mention completely unfair. Molly had always encouraged her customers to consider themselves right at home when they came to the Cut. It had been part of her business plan from the first, to make a place where women could come and let it all hang out. No subject was—or ever had been—off-limits. It was because of the talk that went on at the Cut that Molly had decided to run for mayor. And it was due to the support of the very women who wouldn't shut up about her and Tate that she had won the election. Uh-uh. She refused to go changing her own rules just because she was the one on the hot seat now.

So she exerted great effort to keep her mouth shut

and her expression agreeable. It wasn't any walk in the park. It wore her down.

She got home at seven to find Granny in her big royal-blue La-Z-Boy chair, a tray in her lap and a paring knife in her hand. She was eating slices of Wisconsin cheddar on saltine crackers. The box the cheese had come out of sat open on the sofa.

"Granny, where did you get the cheese?"

Granny muttered something under her breath and set another slice of cheese on a cracker. Molly picked up the box. It was addressed to Granny, all right. And there was a card.

Best Regards, Tate.

"Oh, Granny. How could you?"

Granny did have the grace to look somewhat contrite—as she popped the snack into her mouth. "Baby hon," she said, after she'd chewed and swallowed, "you know I never could resist a good cheddar. It came at four. I didn't know it was from *him.* So I opened it. I saw the card at the same time that I saw it was cheese. Well, sweetie, I cannot bring myself to throw away a fine big block of cheese. It's just not in me. I'm sorry, but it's not." Granny cut herself a fresh slice and set it neatly on another cracker.

Molly stood there, watching her granny chew. It occurred to her that Dixie must have had that talk with Tate—and that she should have told her mother more firmly not to do that.

But then again, well, Granny did look so contented, sitting there chomping away, with bits of cracker stuck to her lip. Granny rarely got gifts—especially this kind of gift, appearing out of the blue and obviously chosen for her and her alone.

"You mad at me?" asked Granny sheepishly after she'd swallowed.

"Oh, Granny. It's only that I thought you hated that man."

"Well, sure I do. I hate *all* men."

"But then what are you doing eating something he sent you?"

Granny shrugged. "Angel heart, if you'll just give me back my shotgun, I'll blow that Tate's head off. But you really can't ask me to say no to cheese."

Chapter Six

The cheese was only the beginning.

To Tate's mind, Dixie had shown up at his door at exactly the right moment—about the time he was actually starting to doubt if he would ever claim Molly for his bride. What Dixie had suggested made a whole lot of sense to him. If Molly wouldn't let him near her, he would begin to move in on her by getting good and friendly with those she loved.

And not only her shotgun-happy granny. Tate decided he would take Dixie's advice and run with it. The day that Granny got the cheese, Tate had Miranda call Jim-Denny's Diner and find out what days Dixie worked.

"Six to two, Tuesday through Saturday," Miranda reported, and Tate then told her that until further notice, he wouldn't be needing breakfast on those days.

He pushed through Jim-Denny's glass door at eight the next morning. A hush kind of fell over the place for a few seconds there. But then Dixie, delivering an armful of orders at one of the back tables, called out, "Tate! How are you, hon? Grab yourself a seat, and I'll be right there." The dead-on stares turned to sideways glances and the talking recommenced—if with something of a furtive, gossipy quality.

Ray Deekins, Dixie's unemployed fiancé, was sitting down at the end of the counter, so Tate strolled over and took the stool next to him.

"How you doing there, Ray?" he asked as he reached for the laminated menu stuck in the holder behind the napkin dispenser.

"Well, Tate, I'm just fine." Ray, a rangy fellow with a retiring manner, dipped his sandy-brown head and sipped from his coffee. A minute later, Dixie slid in behind the counter. She filled Tate's cup and took his order, all the while smiling that gorgeous smile of hers.

While Dixie was scratching on her order pad, Tate glanced over at Ray. He was looking at Dixie as if she hung the damn moon. For some mysterious reason, that look on Ray's face had Tate thinking of Molly—and that embarrassed him.

He quickly looked away, his gaze settling on the smoke-stained yellow wall opposite the counter. A series of old photos hung there, photos of the long-dead Jim-Denny himself. In each picture, Jim-Denny stood on the bank of a muddy lake or a pond and proudly held up a flathead catfish. More than one of those fish was as big as a Saint Bernard.

"He was a noodler, old Jim-Denny was," Ray said, noticing the direction of Tate's gaze.

"We'll have this order right up, Tate." Dixie winked at him and then bounced on over and stuck Tate's order under the wire above the grill.

"Jim-Denny was an Oklahoman by birth," Ray continued in a musing tone. "Hands all scarred up from sticking his fists in the mud banks of bogs..."

Tate already knew this, but he didn't let on. He sat there and drank his coffee and listened to Ray tell him all about the ancient art of noodling, where fishermen used their own hands as bait.

"The world is one wild place, ain't it?" Ray asked rhetorically after he'd finished the tale.

Tate agreed that it was. "Looking for work, are you, Ray?" He gestured at the want ads open in front of Ray.

"Well, I am considering it," Ray replied modestly. "Work just exhausts me, I won't kid you. I don't have the concentration or the disposition for it and I never did." Ray lowered his voice and spoke confidentially. "But I figure I ought to do something, now that Dixie has said she will be my wife. She works hard. I know I owe it to her to help out."

"Good point," agreed Tate. Ray's inability to hold a job was the next thing to legend around town. Folks liked to say he hadn't worked in decades. But Tate, who made it his business to keep up with what went on in his town, knew that now and then, Ray would manage to get himself hired on somewhere. Inevitably he would miss a lot of days—or while on the job, his attention would wander. He'd always ended up fired.

"Hey, if you hear of anyone hiring, maybe you

could let me know?'' Ray looked at him kind of half-hopefully—as if he wasn't really sure himself about the whole concept of joining the workaday world.

Since Tate—and Tucker, too, technically—owned a percentage of most of the businesses in town, Tate had a pretty good idea of who might be looking to hire a new man.

Would that help his cause with Molly, if he arranged for Ray to get work? Hell. Doing something like that was against his most firmly held beliefs. Forcing one of the local merchants to hire Ray would be, beyond a doubt, bad for business.

And Tate Bravo did not do what was bad for business.

To what depths was he willing to sink to get Molly to give in and marry him? It was a question he decided to ponder further at a later time. ''Sure, Ray,'' he said in a tone that made no promises.

About then, Dixie set Tate's breakfast in front of him. She leaned in close, and he got a whiff of her heady perfume. ''Got a call from you-know-who last night. Can you believe someone sent my mama five pounds of Wisconsin cheddar yesterday?''

Tate felt a warmth inside, a sensation of self-satisfaction. ''Did your mama enjoy it?''

Dixie nodded. ''She was tuckin' into it good and proper when you-know-who got home from work.'' Dixie leaned a little closer and lowered her voice another notch. ''So what's next?''

''Still deciding,'' Tate replied mysteriously. ''That's a big, long list you gave me, and I have plenty of choices.''

Dixie beamed. "Well, keep it up. I think you just might be on the right track."

Saturday, it was candy corn. Granny was happily munching away when Molly got home from the shop and a little last-minute grocery shopping at four.

"From Tate?" Molly asked, though she already knew the answer.

Granny nodded. "Honey bunch, what could I do? It's candy corn."

"Buy your own?" Molly suggested hopefully.

Granny only grunted and grabbed another handful. And on Sunday?

Granny got barbecue—delivered straight from that great place out on the highway. Now, how had he done that? Molly wondered. That place on the highway was closed on Sundays.

And however he'd managed to get those fall-right-off-the-bone ribs on Sunday, they weren't all of it. Tate sent the full array of fixings, too: a choice of hot or mild sauce, tart and sweet slaw, foam cups full of both baked beans and string beans, pillow-soft potato rolls…

There was even a half pound of brisket and two hot links.

"Sweet love, you have got to have some of this," Granny insisted when the feast arrived.

Molly didn't even bother to argue. After all, she liked her barbecue, too. And if Tate wanted to kiss up to Granny, well, that was a good thing, wasn't it?

Just because Molly refused to marry Tate didn't mean she wouldn't do what she could to build a cordial relationship with him. She would try her best to get along with him, though in the end, she had doubts she would succeed. On every front—political, sexual and matrimonial—she'd set herself to subverting his famous iron will. Tate didn't take kindly to anyone who subverted of his will.

While they were sucking the rib meat off the bone and forking up big mouthfuls of beans and slaw, Granny looked across the table and asked, "You having his baby, sweetie love?"

"How'd you hear that?" Molly said carefully. In the past four years, since she'd had that accident at the iron foundry and taken early retirement, Granny didn't get out much.

"Word gets around, sugar, even to those of us who keep close to home. And the word is you're pregnant and you have refused Tate Bravo's offer of marriage."

Molly swallowed a bite of tender brisket. "Oh, Granny. It was no offer, it was a flat-out command."

"So, it's true, then." Granny let out a gleeful cackle of laughter.

"You've got barbecue sauce on your chin—and what are you laughing about?"

Granny grabbed a napkin. "Well, dear heart, after two generations of disappearing men, it's downright refreshing to see an O'Dare woman finally meet up with a man who is plumb determined to do what is right."

Molly wasn't feeling all that refreshed. "Look at you. A week ago, you were firing your shotgun at him."

"You know very well I fired way over his head— and now that you mention it, where *is* my shotgun?"

"Safe."

"Safe where?"

"Forget that shotgun. Consider your pride and your dignity. A little barbecue and some candy corn and Tate Bravo's got you eating out of his hand."

Granny did more cackling. "Don't forget the cheese."

Molly was not the least amused. "I'm not marrying him. Don't think I will. It would never work out."

"Darling love, I know you'll do what you have to do. Pass me some more of those green beans, now will you?"

Monday Granny received two digitally remastered Bob Wills and the Texas Playboys CDs. When Molly got home, "Big Ball's in Cowtown" blared from the stereo and Granny was dancing around the room.

"Granny!" Molly shouted over the fiddles and guitars. "Don't you think this is going a little too far?"

"I sure do love those Texas Playboys," Granny shouted back. "When I was a little thing, Mama and Daddy used to pile me in the pickup and take off to dance halls all over the state. I'd fall asleep in the balcony to the sweet rockin' sounds of Western swing. Oh, my. Oh, yes..." Granny closed her eyes and went on dancing.

Tuesday, when Molly came home, Tate was right there, bold as you pleased, with a leg up on her porch railing, making himself good and comfortable. Granny sat in the rocker holding a picture frame tight to her chest.

"Granny, are you crying?" Molly blinked in disbelief as she watched a single tear trail down her grandmother's creased brown cheek. Granny sniffed, waved a hand and looked off toward the pecan tree beside the porch. "Granny?" Granny pressed her lips together, shook her head and clutched the picture frame tighter.

Ignoring the thrill that shivered through her at the sight of him, Molly turned to Tate. "What did you do to her?"

"Hello, Molly," he said, as if challenging her to observe the proprieties.

He was getting no civilities from her until she damn well knew what was happening here. "Why is my granny crying?"

Granny spoke up then. "Oh, honey cakes, I'm not crying because I'm sad. I'm crying because...well, Tate has brought me something today that I didn't even know I wanted. Just look here." She peeled the picture frame off her chest and turned it Molly's way.

It held a glossy studio photo of a chubby, goofy-looking cowboy with a space between his teeth. "Andy Devine," Molly muttered. Granny had always been a huge fan of Andy Devine.

"And look there," Granny cried with a sniff. "Autographed, too." Granny grabbed the picture back and hugged it some more. "Oh, where are all the men like Andy? I always did love him. Agreeable and down-to-earth and loyal as they come. From *The Spirit of Notre Dame* to *Wild Bill Hickock* and *Andy's Gang.* He was even in *Stagecoach,* remember that?" Warily Molly nodded. Granny heaved a big sigh. "Dead and gone over twenty-five years now. Where does the time go?" Granny dashed a second tear away and gazed adoringly at the long-gone Andy's glossy image. "I'm hanging this in my bedroom where I'll see it first thing in the morning and last thing at night. It never hurts to be reminded of things as they should be, or the things that can bring a smile." She threw back her head and crowed, "Hey, Wild Bill, wait for me!" Then she jumped from the rocker, yanked open the storm door and disappeared inside.

Molly gave Tate a sideways look. "I'm beginning to think she really ought to get out more."

He shrugged. "It made her happy. What's wrong with that?"

She looked at him for a long time, thinking how handsome he was, with those fine broad shoulders and those sexy dark eyes. Finally she realized that good manners required a few appreciative words. It wasn't easy, after all their wrangling, to speak to him pleasantly. But somehow, she managed it.

"It's nice that you've been...good to Granny. She's loved everything you sent her. I know you had a few clues from my mother. But still, Granny doesn't get enough attention, and you have given her pleasure. And for that, I do thank you."

He had that look about him. As if he would like to grab her and gobble her up. The problem was, Molly realized, she wouldn't mind being gobbled one bit. Not as long as the one doing the gobbling was Tate. "Come on," he said.

She eyed him uneasily. "Come on, where?"

"Let me take you to Junction Steakhouse. We'll get ourselves a couple of T-bones." He smiled then. Oh, Lordy, that man did have one killer of a smile—when he chose to use it.

Molly sank to the rocker that Granny had vacated. She felt just a little bit shaky, she truly did. "It's just so strange…"

"Tell me." His voice was soft as cottonwood fluff, blowing light on the evening air.

"To have you sitting right there on my porch rail, asking me out. I'm not used to it. It's just…not the way things have been between us."

He gave her an easy shrug. "Well, Molly. It's one of the benefits of everyone knowing about us. Since we're not sneaking around anymore, we can spend an evening together and not care who finds out. They all know, anyway."

It sounded lovely. For a second or two. But then she considered a little more deeply. "Yeah, and when they do find out I had dinner with you—I mean, if I *do* have dinner with you—I'll never hear the end of it."

"Ignore all the gossip," he instructed, as if it were that simple.

"I'm doing my best—and while I'm ignoring the gossip, what should I do about the never-ending criticism and the steady stream of thoughtful advice?"

"Tune it out."

She snapped her fingers. "Just like that, huh?"

"That's right."

"Easy for you to say," she muttered.

"Hey, they gossip about me, too."

"Yeah, but I'll bet not a one of them has the nerve to tell you what they think of you right to your face."

He frowned—and then he got an amused kind of look. "And just what *do* they think of me?"

"You don't want to hear." She was muttering again.

He leaned closer still. "Molly." His dark eyes made promises she longed to let him keep. "Please. Have dinner with me."

Whoa, Molly thought. *Just a darn minute,* now. She folded her arms under her breasts and rocked to the rhythm of her own frustration. "Smooth. Real smooth. When we both know what you did in my salon last week—shouting it out like that, making total fools of both of us."

He gave her a look she could have taken as patronizing. But then again, maybe not. Maybe that look was a tender one. "You did say to go ahead," he reminded her, "that everyone would have to know eventually anyway."

She rocked some more. "Put it in pretty paper, tie it up with a big, shiny bow. Dress it up any way you want to, but that's not going to change what you did, let alone *why* you did it. You tried to use shouting out the truth about the baby as a threat to get me in line—and when your threat didn't work, you were cornered. You had to go through with the shouting part."

He shifted on the porch rail, leaning back and then leaning close again. "Say I told you I regret that I did go through with it, that I am sincerely sorry for any pain or emotional suffering I have caused you by announcing outright what you weren't yet ready to make public knowledge."

She resisted the powerful urge to reach out and touch his handsome face. Sourly she challenged,

"What kind of piddly little apology is that? Are you sorry or not?"

"I *am,* Molly." His voice was as smooth and intoxicating as the expensive whiskey he liked to drink. "I am deeply sorry for any pain or emotional suffering I have *ever* caused you."

She set to rocking again—much more gently than before. At last, she nodded. "All right, then. Apology accepted."

His smile was knowing and sexy and made her long to launch herself into his arms, lock her mouth to his and proceed to do the very things that had gotten them into this fix in the first place. "Well, then." His voice was Tupelo honey now, flowing out sweet and slow. "Would you have dinner with me?"

Suspicion flared, searing away her tender, yearning feelings. She rocked back hard in her chair. "Wait a minute. I get it. This is just more of the same, isn't it? You're just working on me to get me to go out with you—so you can work on me some more to get me to marry you. You're not really sorry for shouting out the news about the baby, and you never were."

His eyes kind of sparked, betraying his temper, which she knew from hard experience was as hot as her own. But he didn't lose it. He spoke again, so gently. "Molly. I *am* sorry." He put up a hand, palm out, like a witness taking an oath. "I swear it. I am sorry. Won't you please believe me?"

She had to admit that he did look at least somewhat regretful—and her throat felt tight. She cleared it. "Okay. I accept your apology."

"Thank you." He granted her a regal nod. Then he turned his head half-away and slid her a glance.

"However, I think to be fair you ought to apologize to me, too."

She stopped rocking and stuck out her chin at him. "*I* should apologize? For what?"

He made a sound halfway between a grunt and a chuckle. "Maybe you've forgotten how you snuck in my window, woke me from a sound sleep, told me you were pregnant and then climbed right out the window again?"

Molly lifted a hand from the chair arm and studied her manicure. The polish on one nail had a tiny nick in it. "I admit. I should've found a better way to tell you."

Nobly he replied, "I accept your apology."

Had it been an apology? Well, if technically it hadn't been, she was willing to allow that her way of telling him about the baby hadn't been any more considerate than *his* way of telling everyone else. She acknowledged his acceptance with a nod fully as regal as his had been. She also knew his next question before he asked it.

"All right, then. Dinner?"

Her contrary nature had her pretending to hesitate—but not for long. She looked down at her Prime Cut T-shirt and then back up at him. "Give me five minutes?"

The gleam of triumph flared in his eyes. "Five minutes it is."

They ate at Tres Erisos, the private club behind Junction Steakhouse. At Tres Erisos, members could purchase drinks by the glass. Tate liked a glass of his high-dollar whiskey before dinner.

"Texas," Molly muttered, shaking her head, when their waitress, Adela, set Tate's drink in front of him.

He saluted Molly and took a sip. "No place like it," he announced with pride, setting down his glass.

"Ain't that the truth," she grumbled, glancing around at the other booths and at the U-shaped mahogany bar in the center of the dim room. Everywhere she looked, pairs of avid eyes quickly looked away. "You'd think we could at least all agree on our liquor laws." In Texas, as in many southern states, some counties were "dry." You could not buy liquor in any form. Most counties, like theirs, were "partially dry;" liquor was available but carefully controlled. A few were "wet," which meant restaurants and bars could be licensed to serve drinks and you didn't have to drive miles and miles to find a package liquor store.

Tate was frowning. "What's the problem now? You want a drink?"

"No, I don't. And that's not my point."

He took another sip—a big one. "I'll take that to mean you do *have* a point."

"Ha-ha."

"Molly." He seemed to be keeping his voice low with effort. "If you want to change the liquor laws, better run for county supervisor."

"I'm not through as mayor yet."

"Did you have to remind me?" He signaled Adela for another. She set it in front of him almost before he got his hand in the air. Molly scowled. "What?" he demanded.

"Oh, nothing." She fiddled with the stem of her water glass. "I don't usually hang around in private drinking clubs with the good ol' boys, that's all."

"Molly," he said again. That was all. Just *Molly,* in a weary, worldly-wise, so-patient tone.

"Tres Erisos. What is that? Doesn't *eriso* mean 'hedgehog' or something?"

"Yes, Molly. I believe it does."

"Well, then, I've always wondered—what's that about? Three Hedgehogs? We don't have hedgehogs in Texas. Three Rattlesnakes. That's what they should have called this place."

Tate said nothing. He only looked at her, patient as Job.

Was she being the *itch*-word that began with a *b?* Oh, probably. "All right, all right." She made herself sit up a little straighter.

He looked at her from under lowered brows. "You keep sighing like that, you'll blow the dishes right off the table."

"Sorry…" What was she doing here? What was the point? "I mean it." She leaned in and spoke in a whisper. "I'm not marrying you, so don't think, since I let you buy me dinner, that I will."

He drank more whiskey. "Correct me if I'm wrong, but I do believe you said that before."

She slumped back in her chair. "I'm just afraid that you're not listening, that's all."

"Pick up your menu," he ordered softly. "Decide what you'll have."

For once, she didn't take issue with his commanding ways. She opened her menu, scanned the choices and set it back down. "Okay, I'm ready."

At a mere glance from Tate, Adela hustled over. They ordered. Their salads arrived and their steaks soon after. They ate in silence—well, once or twice

Tate tried to revive the dead-and-buried conversation, but Molly only shook her head and cut another bite of steak.

As Adela removed their plates, the waitress attempted to brightly inquire, "Desser—?"

"No, thanks," Molly replied before Adela even got that second syllable out of her mouth. After Tate signed the check and laid down a big cash tip, they were out of there.

His Cadillac waited at the curb, gleaming in the fading light of the glorious purple-and-pink Texas sunset. He ushered her over to it and pulled open the passenger door. Molly didn't duck inside. She stood frozen on the sidewalk, staring at that open door. There was…a tightness around her chest, had been since the moment she'd taken the seat across the table from him in Tres Erisos. It was all so strange, to be openly sharing a meal with Tate, right out in public for anyone to see, and now to be standing on Center Street, bold as you please, about to climb inside his big, fancy car. Never had she believed anything like this would happen.

Feelings of yearning and loss, of hope and mistrust swirled around in her. Those feelings were not comfortable ones. They tightened her stomach, made her heart beat fast and hurtfully under her ribs.

"Just get in," he said. "Please."

She opened her mouth to say something rude—but then changed her mind. Really, he'd been a perfect gentleman all evening. Maybe that was what scared her the most.

"Please," he said again, low and way too careful that time.

Since she couldn't think of a single valid reason not to, she stepped up and slid inside. He shut the door and went around and got behind the wheel.

They drove to her place without speaking. He stopped the car at the foot of her long driveway—and turned off the engine and the headlights. This was it, and she knew it. He was going to start in about how she had to marry him, and she wasn't sitting still for that.

She leaned on her door, a hasty thank-you rising to her lips.

He spoke before she could. "What's it gonna take?"

On the thousand-to-one chance he wasn't talking about her marrying him, she asked, "To…?"

He was staring straight ahead, into the evening-shadowed trees that lined the driveway. He lifted one big shoulder in a half shrug. "To get you to talk to me? To get you to cut me a half an inch of slack?" He sounded so…hurt. Hurt and kind of lost and for-lorn.

The scariest thing happened to her then. She felt tenderness. Toward Tate. It was warm and it was sweet and it was flooding all through her. She gulped. "I…well, we got in the club and I just didn't want to be there."

"You could have said so."

"And if I had?"

"We'd have got up and left."

She shook her head. "I'd said I'd go out with you. I wanted to keep my word. But I was having second thoughts."

"About going to dinner with me?" he asked,

though it really wasn't a question. "Yeah," he said and made a low, pained sound, eyes straight ahead. "I got that message pretty clear."

She shifted in the plush leather seat, so she was facing him more fully. "We aren't suited. You know we're not. You're forever barking orders—and I'm not a woman to do what any man tells me to. I'm not going to marry you, Tate. You have to believe me. It would be a disaster for both of us, not to mention for our innocent child."

He looked at her then, a hot kind of look that burned right through her. "Have I said one damn word about marriage this whole god-awful evening?"

She looked down at her hands. "No. But I know you're going to. I keep waiting for the other boot to drop."

"Then you can *stop* waiting. It's not going to happen."

Hope rose within her. "You mean you're not going to bring it up?"

"Not tonight, that's for damn certain."

"Promise?"

"On the graves of my ancestors." He looked very serious—even bleak.

And suddenly, she was giggling. "You mean that? You swear on all four generations of Tucker Tates?"

He nodded. "Every hard-nosed one of them." The bleak look had faded. Now, she could almost swear she saw a smile trying to pull at the corners of his mouth.

She allowed, "I guess you've convinced me."

"Good." He did smile then. And somehow, she realized, they had both leaned toward each other across the console. The scent of him came to her: leather and manliness and pricey aftershave. "Kiss me, Molly," he whispered.

"Um, ahem," she said softly. But she didn't move back.

"Come on. Do it…"

"Tate…"

"Kiss me…"

That tenderness she'd been feeling? It was changing. Growing hotter. Turning molten inside her. Burning into desire. "Tate. The thing is…"

His wonderful lips were very close. She could feel his warm breath across her cheek. "Kiss me."

"You're not, uh, listening."

"Aw, Molly. I am. You just said I wasn't listening. And you said my name. And you said, 'um' and 'uh' and 'ahem.'" He stole a quick one, his lips brushing hers in a searing, too-short caress. "Did I get it right?"

"Oh, you…"

"Did I?"

"Yeah." She smiled. How could she help it? "I guess you pretty much did."

"Now, about that kiss?"

"Tate, I'm not going home with you tonight."

"I know."

"Er…you do?"

He was nodding. "Just a kiss…"

"Oh." She looked at his beautiful mouth. How could she help herself? "Well…"

"What?"

"Yes." It kind of slipped out. And then she wondered…

Had she really said that?

Apparently so. And what was she doing now?

Why, craning across the console.

Such a very short distance. A mere inch or two...

Her lips met his. Molly sighed and so did Tate. He reached out those strong arms and pulled her closer against him. Oh, he smelled so lovely and manly. And his muscled body felt so good against her softer one. And his mouth...

Oh, Lordy. That mouth...

If the console hadn't been in the way, she'd have eagerly scooted right onto his lap.

But it *was* in the way and maybe that was a good thing. It kept them from going beyond his mouth on hers and his tongue sliding, wet and insistent and slightly rough, along the crease where her lips met.

Well, and why not? she asked herself and didn't listen too closely for the answer. She opened, sighing some more. His tongue dipped in and he kissed her deeply as his big hands roamed her back.

Oh, it really was heaven, to be in Tate's arms again. Too much of heaven, it honestly was....

With considerable reluctance, Molly put her palms flat against his hard chest and gave a firm push.

He lifted his head and whispered her name.

She put her fingers against his lips. "Now, why did I do that?" He only grinned. Wouldn't it be nice, she found herself thinking, to sit here forever with his big, strong arms around her? He moved those soft lips, nibbling on the tip of her middle finger. Really, now, how could those lips of his be so soft—when the rest of him was so very, very hard?

Oh, my. Better put a stop to thoughts like that. She

removed her fingers from his mouth and put both hands on his chest again. Gently she pushed. He let her go.

Say something. Now, she ordered herself. "Uh. Sorry I gave you such a hard time at dinner." It came out in the most ridiculous, breathy, yearning little whisper.

Time to go and then some. She felt for the door handle behind her.

He sent her a look that melted her midsection. "Make it up to me."

She was not going to ask. "How?"

"Dinner and a movie. Friday night. We can go into Abilene."

"Abilene?" She repeated the word as if she'd never heard of the place.

"What time can you be ready?"

She shouldn't answer that. "I could, uh, be home by six…"

"I'll pick you up at six-thirty."

"Er, six forty-five?" Now, how had *that* slipped out?

"Six forty-five, it is," he confirmed with a nod.

Dinner and a movie, she thought dazedly. Dinner and a movie with Tate. Friday night.

Had she just agreed to that?

Oh, yes, she had. And though his mouth was silent, his eyes were still talking. And the things they were saying…

Oh, my. She licked her lips and he watched her do that, his sexy grin widening and those dark eyes sparking with heat.

If she didn't get out of that car immediately, who

knows what kind of promises she'd be making him next?

"Molly…" His eyes offered all manner of delights if she'd only scoot back over there toward the driver's side.

"Uh, Tate."

"Um?"

"You know, I've really got to go in."

He frowned. "But it's not even nine o'clock."

"Yeah. But…uh. It's Tuesday. A work night. I need, you know, a good night's sleep. So. Gotta go."

He caught her hand then. She blinked and stared as he raised it to his lips and kissed the back of it and a shimmer of heated wonder spread all through her, starting at the point where his mouth touched her skin.

Now, how did he do it? A tender touch. The brush of his lips against the back of her hand…

And she was putty. Mush. A pitiful puddle of molten desire.

"Gotta go," she whispered, as if she hadn't already said it several times before.

"Good night, then." He actually released her hand.

Now, she thought. *Go. Now.* She leaned on her door so hard, it popped wide open. Her upper body kind of fell out into the silky, humid evening air. "Oops." She let out a silly, throaty giggle and pulled herself back into the seat, beaming Tate one last wide, dazed smile. "Uh. Bye."

"Bye, Molly."

She swung her feet to the ground and stood. Her knees wobbled at first, but then she remembered to stiffen them. Quickly, before she could find an excuse to jump back in that car with him, she shut the door and hurried off into the gathering dark, hustling fast toward the safety of her own little house.

Tate watched her go, smiling. ''Molly, Molly, Molly,'' he whispered under his breath. There was, apparently, much to be said for what Dixie had called *courting mode*.

Things were looking up. Yes, indeed. They certainly were.

Chapter Seven

As expected, Molly received more than her share of criticism and advice the next day. By noon, everyone knew that she'd been to Tres Erisos with Tate.

"I think it's a good thing, Molly. He is the father of your baby and whatever happens, it's important that you try to be on speaking terms with him."

"Don't like it. Hated to hear it. Did you know he's been hanging around at the diner, too? Makin' up to Dixie and that Ray? I'm beginning to think that man will stop at nothing to bend you to his will."

"Watch out, Molly. He'll be sliding a diamond on your finger before you know it."

"Oh, Molly. I know you'll end up marrying him. Isn't it romantic? Tate Bravo. Hunka, hunka."

Strangely, she was finding, all the interest in her private life didn't bother her as much since last night.

Maybe it had to do with being on slightly better terms with Tate.

And no, she did not plan to marry the man—no matter what any of them thought. But it did make her feel better, that she and Tate had managed to talk for a while without shouting at each other. That tense and awful as their dinner had been, at least it had been right out in public, proudly and with dignity. No slinking around and no lying to anyone.

As for that kiss they'd shared…

Well, it was only one. And she would watch herself on Friday. She was not going to end up in his bed, naked and moaning and begging for more….

"Molly, sweetie pie, it's getting in my eyes."

"Oops." She grabbed a towel and handed it to Emmie so she could dab the Serendipitous Sable 4 out of her left eye.

"You were daydreaming, weren't you?" Emmie accused, both eyes narrowed now. "Daydreaming about—"

Molly didn't let her say it. "I certainly was not. Now sit still, and let me finish you up."

When Molly got home, Granny had Bob Wills blaring. She stood in front of the brass-framed mirror that hung over the living room's miniscule mantel, admiring herself in a brand-new brown leather bomber jacket.

Molly grabbed the remote and turned the music down enough that the windows stopped rattling. "I guess I don't need to ask where that jacket came from."

Granny turned her back to the mirror and sent a

flirty glance over her shoulder. "My, oh my, I do look good, now don't I? You notice the resemblance?"

Molly folded her arms and tapped a foot. "What are you talking about?"

"Come on, honey love. It's obvious. Stop and look. Really look."

Grudgingly Molly did. And what do you know? "Butter my butt and call me a biscuit. Amelia Earhart."

"You got it."

Molly couldn't help grinning. "You *do* look like her. You truly do." Granny had the same short wavy hair—with maybe a touch more gray in it. And the face...

No doubt about it. Amelia Earhart, with an extra wrinkle or two.

"She was before my time, acourse. But I've seen the pictures." Granny turned to the mirror again and lifted her chin high, stretching out all signs of sagging. "In my most secret heart, I have always dreamed of flight..."

All unbidden, Molly felt a knot of emotion tighten her throat. She swallowed it. "Kind of hot out for leather, though."

Granny sent her a reproachful look. "No sour grapes, now, sugar plum."

Molly blew out a breath. "You're right. I'm sorry." She added softly, "You look just like her, you honestly do."

Granny turned right and then left, and then fiddled with the collar. "Gonna get me some of those wide-legged pleated pants with the cuffs on them. I think I will do that. I definitely will."

* * *

Tate rang the doorbell right on time.

Granny got there first and flung the door wide. "Tate!" she exclaimed with such glee and excitement, you would have thought Andy Devine had climbed from the grave, freshened up a little and come to call. "Come on in." She pushed the storm door open and he stepped through, all spit and polish in tan slacks and a dark polo shirt.

"Dusty." He granted Granny one of those slow, sexy smiles of his. "You do look handsome in that jacket."

Granny preened shamelessly. "Well now, I do, don't I? And what's this?" He handed her a small brown bag. She peeked inside. "Candy corn. Now, how did you know I was just about out?"

Tate made a low, modest noise in his throat. "I had a feeling you might be running low."

They ate at Spanos, where the fine food and service inside belied the strip-mall exterior. They talked and laughed together, sharing a new ease that made everything fun. Tate had chicken parmesan, and Molly cleaned up her plate of shrimp primavera—leaving so little room in her stomach, she was forced to say no when it came time for dessert.

Tate ordered Chocolate Wonderful, Spano's famous chocolate-cinnamon Bundt cake with hot fudge sauce and whipped cream.

She watched him eat it and teased him about Granny. "I know what you're doing. You are buttering up my granny."

He put on a noble face. "She's the baby's great-grandma. Of course I'm going to treat her right.'' Now, why did that make her silly heart beat faster? He offered her a bite. She looked at the tempting bit of fudge-drizzled cake extended toward her on his fork. ''Have some,'' he said in a voice that sent hot shivers slithering up and down her spine.

How could she resist? She opened her mouth and he slid that fork in, the tines kind of kissing the top of her tongue, the cake and hot fudge sauce instantly melting.

Oh, it was heavenly. She tasted the dreamy mingling of sweet flavors and swallowed. Then she smoothed her napkin. ''That's enough of that, now.'' She sent him a chiding look.

He already had another bite ready. And the look in his eyes... ''Just one more,'' he coaxed.

Snap out of it, she silently commanded herself. A woman should have sense enough not to eat right off a man's fork—that is, not unless she was sending him a seductive message about what she intended to be nibbling on later.

Uh-uh. Molly wouldn't be doing any nibbling of that nature. She shook her head.

The hot light in his eyes faded a little, but he didn't press the issue.

The movie was one of those heist flicks. Lots of action and high-tech burglar devices and beautiful actresses in slinky evening dresses. Molly enjoyed it. And when Tate's hand settled gently on hers, she couldn't quite bring herself to push it away. By the time the hero kissed the beautiful movie star in the red sequined evening gown, Molly had twined her fingers with Tate's.

They drove home through the sultry night. Tate had some soft music on the CD player and the beautiful, powerful car hummed along the highway.

When he pulled in at the bottom of her driveway, turned off the engine and switched out the lights, she found she had a problem.

She didn't want to get out. She didn't want the lovely night to end.

"We could go on out to the ranch," he suggested softly through the darkness.

How had he known what she shouldn't have been thinking? "Bad idea."

"Why?"

"You know why. And why do you always park at the foot of the driveway?"

He grinned, white teeth gleaming through the dimness. "Good question. No reason for it, really—now you hid Dusty's shotgun."

"Oh, cut it out. Even if I gave her back that gun, she'll never point it at you again, and you know it. Never thought I'd see the day, but in the short span of a week and a half, you have broken her down good and proper. She's putty in your hands now, and don't try to kid me that you haven't noticed."

"You're not happy that she likes me now?" He sounded a little bit hurt.

She started to reel off a snappish answer and then stopped herself. Solemnly she told him, "I know it's a good thing. You said it yourself earlier. She's the baby's great-granny and it's best if the two of you can get along."

"And what about us, Molly?" His voice had gone

low, with an intimate roughness. "Isn't it best if we get along, too?"

She felt way too defensive suddenly. "Yeah, it is—which is why I'm out on a date with you."

He was quiet for a moment. When he spoke, his voice was even lower and more intimate than before. "And is that the only reason you're out with me? Because of the baby, because you think we should get along?"

It wasn't, of course—though she almost wished that it could have been. Things would have been so much simpler if only she didn't constantly dream of the way his big arms felt when they were close around her. "You're working me, Tate. You know you are. And I should go in now. Thanks for a wonderful dinner and the—"

He cut in. "Stay." Now he sounded so tender, so full of hope and yearning. Her heart melted. "Just for a minute or two," he whispered.

"I really shouldn't—" The sentence stopped dead as he reached across and took her arm.

She gasped as heat flared from the point of contact, rushing up her shoulder, flooding down over her breasts, into her belly—and lower still. How did he do this to her? "Oh, Tate…" Her voice came out husky, full of need and confusion.

"Stay." He pulled her close.

She resisted—but it was no good. She wanted to kiss him. And he was right there, ready, willing and able to give her just what she wanted. She let it happen, let him pull her to him, until her hip pressed the console and she couldn't get closer.

"Molly," he whispered, with a yearning and a frustration to match her own.

"Oh, Tate…" Their lips met and his arms crushed her close.

Yes, she thought as his tongue toyed with hers. *Oh my, yes.*

She let out a tiny groan as he tugged at the silky shirt she wore, getting it out of her tight jeans so he could touch her bare skin. He caressed her, those knowing fingers sliding over the hot flesh of her lower back, inching upward.

She felt his thumb at her bra strap, teasingly slipping beneath it, and then sliding back and forth. In a second, he would unhook it. He might be a rich man who'd never done hard labor in his life, but when it came to getting a woman's clothes off, Tate had a real talent with his hands…

No. Uh-uh. This had to stop.

She pulled away—well, yanked away really.

"Come back here." His eyes were low-lidded. Oh, this was trouble.

She frantically tucked her shirt back in. "Thanks again. It was a great evening. But I have to go in."

"No, you don't." It came out a low growl.

"Good night." She jerked on the door latch and leaped to her feet, giving the door a hard slam and setting off up the dark driveway at a fast clip. She wore high-heeled sandals and twice she stumbled in her haste to get away from him—and more than from him, from the stunning power of her longing for him.

Somehow, she managed not to look back once. Not even when he gunned the engine and turned on the headlights, sending a blinding wash of revealing light spilling all around her. She thought he would follow her right up to her door.

But he only reversed and drove off, leaving her in the dark with the soft golden gleam of her own porch light up ahead.

He called the next day, early, as she was getting ready to head over to the Cut for her five-hour Saturday shift. Granny picked up the kitchen extension when the phone rang. "Sweetie pie, it's for you!"

"Who is it?" she called back, as if she didn't know.

"Tate!"

"I'll take it in my room." She set her mascara wand on the side of the sink and turned the corner to her bedroom. "You can hang up now, Granny," she said into the phone. Nothing. "Granny?"

"Oh. Well. Sure enough. Bye now, Tate."

"Bye, Dusty."

Molly waited. Still the click didn't come. "Granny," she said in a warning tone.

"All right, all right." The disconnecting click came at last.

Tate got straight to the point. "Come out to the ranch. We'll have a picnic."

"Today?"

"Yeah."

"I can't. I have to work."

"Tomorrow, then."

She wanted to go to him. Way too much. But she'd spent most of the night awake, thinking. If she didn't plan to marry Tate—which she didn't—she shouldn't be dating him. Not when she knew that he was asking

her out with the aim of coaxing her into saying *I do.*
"Tate, I can't."

"Can't tomorrow?"

"I mean, we've got to stop this."

"Stop…?"

"This. You and me. Going out."

"No, we don't."

"We do. It's just…not fair to you."

He was silent—but not for long. "Since when did
you start deciding what's fair to me?"

"Since you think you're going to talk me into marrying you—and *I* know you're not."

The line was quiet again. At last he said softly,
"You afraid, Molly?" His voice poured in her ear,
sweet and rough and heady as homemade berry wine.

She cleared her throat. "Afraid of what?"

"That maybe I'll end up convincing you to do the
right thing, after all?"

She clutched the phone tighter, as if holding on
might protect her from the certainty in his tone. "You
won't convince me of anything—and getting married
isn't necessarily the right thing. Not for everybody."

"I'm not talking about everybody. I'm talking
about you and me and our baby—and you didn't answer my question. Are you afraid?"

"No, I'm not." Oh, but she was. And they both
knew it. "It's just not right, Tate. For me to be dating
you, when I know what you want, and I also know
I'm not going to give it to you."

Yet another silence echoed through the line. One
with a kind of seething quality to it. "Molly?"

"What?"

"Maybe you ought to let me decide what's right for me."

She shook her head vehemently, though he couldn't see her do it. "I don't want to argue about this anymore. It was foolish of me to even try. The point is, I'm not going on a picnic with you tomorrow. I'm not going out with you again, period."

Yet another heartbeat of taut silence elapsed and then, so very softly, he said, "In the end, you will say yes." She almost contradicted him. But no. He hadn't listened when she said no all those other times and she had no reason to hope he might hear her now. He spoke again. "Suppose you tell me, then..."

"Tell you what?"

"Your plan—what exactly is it?"

"My plan?"

"For the future. When the baby comes."

She didn't really like where this was going. Carefully she lowered herself to the edge of her bed. "What do you mean, plan?"

"Are you planning to *allow* him to know his father?"

"I think she's a girl—and yes. Of course you'll know her. I've said from the first that you would."

"When was it you said that? I really don't recall."

Now that he mentioned it, neither did she. "Um, well, whether I said it or not, it's what I've intended. Why else would I have told you, if I didn't mean for you to have a part in her life?"

"Well, Molly, I don't know. Truth is, I don't know why the hell you do half the things you do."

"Don't get insulting or I will hang up this phone."

There was a pause. She could just see him on the

other end, taking slow, careful breaths. Counting to ten...or maybe all the way to twenty. Eventually he tried again. "Joint custody, then? Of *her*—or him. That's what you're planning?"

Joint custody? That meant Tate would get her baby *half* the time? She'd never even considered that. And she couldn't see it working. She had Granny to help her out. What would Tate do? Hire some stranger to look after their child?

Oh, this was awful. She'd never imagined he would want to take any major part in the baby's life. But it sounded as though he did. And what did that mean? In the end, when she still refused to marry him, would he sue her for custody if she argued that he wasn't set up to take care of a child?

She desperately dug around in her mind for the right thing to say—and came up with nothing but the plain truth. "I, well, I haven't really given it a lot of thought yet. I'm not even three months along and there's a plenty of time to—"

He cut her off. "Time? When? If you're not going to see me, how are we going to come to any agreement on how things will be?"

She was sorely tempted to tell him that the two of them were never coming to any agreements, anyway. Never had, never would. But that would not be constructive, and she was doing her level best to be reasonable about this. She told him that, speaking slowly and clearly into the mouthpiece so he wouldn't miss a single word: "I am trying my level best to be reasonable about this."

"You know," he replied, sounding scarily philosophical, "that day at the ranch house, the first time I asked you to marry me—"

"You did not *ask*. You *told*."

"Well, if you want to go nitpicking, I didn't ask *or* tell. You never gave me a damn chance to do either one."

"There was no—"

"As I was saying…" He put heavy emphasis on each word—and then waited, his silence daring her to interrupt again. Oh, she did long to. But she bit her lip and kept her peace. Finally, he continued, "The day I *tried* to ask you to marry me, right before you stormed out on me, you laid it on me good and hard about words like *reasonable* and *right* and *fair.* You said that when I used those words, I only meant we'd be doing things *my* way."

"That's right. I said that. I said it and it's true."

"And exactly what words have *you* been using in the last few minutes, Molly?"

She had a kind of sawdusty dryness in her mouth. "I, uh…"

"What words?"

Busted. "All right. You got me."

He turned the knife a tad. "You used *fair* and *right* and *reasonable.*"

"Okay," she admitted with a heavy sigh.

"And when you used them, you meant that we were going to be doing things *your* way."

"Yeah." She owned up to it. Proudly. No flinching. Because, after all, he had only proved her point. "And that's exactly why we aren't the least suited to each other. I want things *my* way, you want things *your* way. For a relationship to work, someone's got to back down now and then.''

"I can learn to back down.'' He didn't sound especially convincing.

"It's never going to work between us, Tate,'' she cried. "Oh, why can't you see that?''

He immediately changed the subject. "You're just scared. Because when I kiss you, you don't want me to stop.''

She held the phone away from her ear for a second, glared at it, and then flopped back on the bed. "Oh, there is no sense in talking to you…''

"Admit that kissing me scares you.''

"Tate, do you hear me arguing?''

"You admit it then?''

She pressed her lips tight together and glanced at the bedside clock. "I have to be at the salon in twenty minutes.''

"Three little words—'You're right, Tate.'''

Molly closed her eyes and silently counted to ten. "You are impossible.''

"Wrong three words…and Molly?'' She didn't answer. She was considering hanging up on him. But she couldn't quite bring herself to do something so bad-mannered when all he'd done was to tell the truth. "I'm not giving up,'' he said, gently but with absolute determination.

The tender vow echoed in her ear, followed by silence. He had hung up on *her*.

Chapter Eight

Tate stared down at the phone he'd just turned off—
and considered hurling it against the far wall of his
study. He wasn't feeling nearly as gentle or as calm
he'd forced himself to be in that maddening conversation he'd just had with Molly.

I'm not giving up, he'd told her.

Well, damn it. Maybe he *should* give up. Maybe
he should just forget about her *and* their baby.

Then again, he had a grim and sinking feeling that
he would never forget Molly. And no man worthy of
the name forgot his own child. Plus, even if he were
the kind of lowlife no-account who turned his back
on his children, even if he someday managed to put
Molly from his mind, still he'd have a hell of a time
actually forgetting either one of them. In a town the
size of Tate's Junction, it was pretty hard to forget
about anyone for long.

Good enough, then. Instead of forgetting her, he would *ignore* her. He would pretend she wasn't there when he saw her on the street. In town council meetings, he would not address her directly. If anyone mentioned her name to him, he would reply, "Who? Never heard of her." They would all learn fast enough not to dare to speak her name around him.

Regular as clockwork—every blessed month—he would send her a big, fat child-support check. She could cash it or tear it up into itty-bitty pieces. He wouldn't give a damn, either way. Hell, if she didn't take his money, he would invest it, turn it into a Texas-sized nest egg. Eventually he would make sure his kid got the use of it. Molly would burn with resentment that *he* could give their kid more than she could. Let her burn. That would be just fine with Tate.

Yeah. Maybe he would do all that. Oh, yeah. He just might…

Muttering swearwords, Tate turned to the window that looked out over the main porch and the wide, curving driveway beyond it.

Who the hell did he think he was kidding? He wasn't going to do any of those things. He would have Molly yet—and their kid would have married parents, damned if he wouldn't.

Hadn't Tate seen the bad things that growing up with no dad could do to a kid?

You bet he had. Take Molly, for instance. He had to hand it to her, she was strong and smart and she knew how to look after herself. But he'd never met a woman so downright unyielding to the male of the species—him, in particular. She was carrying his baby, she practically went up in flames every time they touched—and he was rich. For your average non-man-hating woman, any one of those reasons would have been more than enough to make her jump at his offer of marriage. Tate was no shrink, but it seemed pretty clear to him that her inability to get along with a man arose from growing up fatherless—from not even knowing who her dad had been.

And what about Tate's own brother, Tucker? Penelope Tate Bravo had always claimed that Tate's dad, the mysterious and long-dead Blake Bravo, was Tucker's father, too. Their grandfather had gone along with that fiction. And if Tucker Tate IV—sometimes known as Ol' Tuck—gave the nod to something, everybody else in a forty mile radius knew damn well they'd better call it right and true. Especially in Ol' Tuck's presence. But according to Tate's mother, Blake Bravo had died out in California while she was pregnant with Tate. So how had a dead man reappeared five years later to sire a second son?

It was a question that both Tucker and Tate were never allowed to ask.

And don't think they hadn't tried. They *had* tried, both of them—when they got old enough to figure out that dead men did not, as a rule, return from the grave. Back then, their questions on the subject were met with vagueness by their mother and distraction by their grandmother.

Tate still remembered what his grandfather had said when Tate drummed up the courage to ask *him*...

"Your mother is a good woman. Are you insulting her?"

"No, Grandfather. I only—"

"Tucker is your brother. Are we clear on that?"

"But—"

"Enough. I see no need to discuss what does not require discussion. We won't be speaking of this again."

And they hadn't. Ever.

Tate always felt kind of sorry for Tucker, that he—like Molly—never even knew who his father might be. At least Tate knew his father's name; at least his mother had married his father. Weren't there those two faded pictures in one of the old family albums of his mother and his long-dead father on their wedding day? His father had his head turned away from the camera in both pictures, so you couldn't see much of his face. But there *was* a marriage license—his grandfather had made certain Tate saw that—so there was no doubt the ceremony *had* taken place.

Growing up, Tate got better treatment from Ol' Tuck than Tucker ever did. And somewhere inside, Tate had always known it was because Ol' Tuck considered him to be the legitimate one. Tucker knew it, too; he and Ol' Tuck never could seem to get along.

And look at Tucker now. Out wandering the world somewhere. Dropping in and out of law school, cut off from his roots.

Hell, no.

Tate wasn't giving up on this. No way *his* kid would be born without his name.

He still had the phone in his hand. Without further hesitation, he punched the talk button.

Molly tapped lightly on the bathroom door. "Granny, you okay in there?"

"I'm fine, sweet stuff. Just fixing my face."

From where she stood in the little square of hall-way, Molly could see into her bedroom, where the morning sun streamed in through the open curtains and her bed was still unmade. The clock on the night-stand said it was ten. Granny had been monopolizing the bathroom for over an hour.

Bewildered, Molly wandered back into the kitchen and poured herself a second cup of decaf. She drib-bled some milk into the decaf, put the carton away and leaned against the counter, sipping thoughtfully.

No doubt about it. Something was up. Granny had been acting strangely since yesterday, when Molly got home from the Cut. Kind of secretive and jumpy.

And now, this morning, fixing her face and taking her sweet time about it... Uh-uh. Granny never primped. She would brush her teeth and run a comb through her hair and that would about do it. Very strange. What in the world could have brought on this sudden attack of extensive grooming?

The doorbell rang. "Would you get that, darlin' child?" Granny sang out from the bathroom. Leaving her mug on the counter, Molly went to answer.

She pulled open the front door and found Tate waiting on the other side of the storm door, wearing Wranglers, a Western shirt and Tony Llama boots— and looking good enough to lick like candy on a stick. She met those coffee-brown eyes through the glass and felt something go hot and hungry down inside.

"Molly," he said softly through the barrier of glass. His expression flat serious, he began looking her over good and slow—from her uncombed hair down over the big Longhorn T-shirt she liked to sleep in, and even lower to the frayed hems of the old shorts she'd pulled on when she got up. He seemed to find her bare legs absolutely spellbinding; he certainly stared at them long enough. And what could possibly be so interesting about her bare feet?

Molly cleared her throat—and she did it loudly enough that he would be sure to hear it through the glass. He took his sweet time dragging his gaze back up to meet her eyes again. Since she wanted to make sure he heard every word of the lecture she intended to deliver, she pushed back the storm door. He stepped over her threshold, and the storm door swung shut behind him.

She backed away. "What are you doing here?" she demanded, ordering the molten heat in her belly to cool off this instant. "I thought I told you I couldn't—"

"Dusty." His sudden wide, friendly smile was aimed over her shoulder.

"Well, good morning," Granny announced from about five feet behind her.

Molly turned around slowly—and blinked twice at what she saw.

Granny looked good. Real good. Her wrinkled cheeks were petal-pink, her lips a muted red and her slightly saggy eyelids had been artfully shadowed. She wore her new bomber jacket, an unfamiliar white shirt underneath it, a tasseled white silk scarf thrown jauntily around her neck and a pair of pleated, wide-legged cream-colored cuffed pants.

When, Molly wondered, had she had time to get that scarf, the shirt and those pants?

Granny must have seen the questions in her eyes.

"Took a little drive into Abilene for some shopping yesterday while you were at work, sugar bun."

"Abilene?" Molly said weakly. Granny so rarely went anywhere. And never all the way to Abilene…

"Dusty," said Tate, still lurking at Molly's back. "You do look mighty fine."

"Why, thank you." Granny glowed with modest pleasure.

Molly tried with all her might to dredge up some moral outrage—that Tate was standing in her living room when she'd told him to stay away. That Granny had never mentioned her trip to Abilene, the clothes she'd bought *or* the fact that Tate, who should have known better, would be showing up this morning. And what about how, as a rule, Molly and Granny always went to church together at eleven? Granny hadn't said a word about how she wouldn't be going today.

But somehow, Molly was having a real problem drumming up even a smidgen of righteous indignation. How could she when she stared into her grandmother's eyes and saw the light of anticipation gleaming there?

Maybe, Molly found herself thinking, this wasn't about missing church. It wasn't about Molly herself, or Tate, or the baby, or even the marriage that was never going to happen.

This was all about Granny. Looking back over the years, Molly couldn't ever remember her grandmother looking half so happy or excited as she did right now.

"Okay," Molly said. "I give. What's going on?"

"Dreams *can* come true, lovey. Tate is taking me flying in his Cessna Skyhawk today."

                        *   *   *

It was past nine that night when Molly heard tires
crunching over the gravel outside. She pointed the
remote at the TV to mute the sound. Tate had better
not push it, she was thinking. Bad enough he'd kept
Granny out all day and half the night. He'd just better
not try anything like coming in for a Coke....

She heard a car door open and shut. And then, dis-
tinctly, she heard Granny call, "Thanks, Tate.
'Night!''

A minute later, Granny came breezing in the door,
her jacket slung over her shoulder and dangling from
a finger. Every star in the sky seemed to be shining
in her eyes.

"Long flight?" Molly asked, keeping her voice
cool and trying not to gape at this new, shining-eyed
granny of hers.

Granny bent close, bringing a smell of candy corn
and red dust. She pressed a big smacking kiss on the
top of Molly's head. "Sweetcakes, have I got some
big news for you." She tossed her jacket on the arm
of the couch, unwound her scarf and dropped it on
the jacket. "I have got myself a job."

Molly turned off the TV. "A job? But I thought
you went flying."

"Oh, I did. And it was grand. But there's more. A
whole lot more..." Granny dropped lightly to the
couch, kicked off her shoes and hiked her legs up to
the side. She braced an arm on the back of the sofa
and canted eagerly toward Molly. "Tate keeps his
plane out at Skinny Jordan's airfield. You remember
Skinny..." Skinny's nickname was no joke. He was
tall and matchstick-thin and about Granny's age.

Around ten years ago, he'd leased some flat, dusty acreage from the Tates, put up a couple of Quonset huts, rolled in a trailer for his ''office'' and started calling it an airfield.

''I know who he is,'' Molly said cautiously.

Granny just glowed. ''Well, good. Skinny and I got to talking, after Tate took me up in the Skyhawk. And then, a while later, Tate said he'd take me up for one more flight. Dear Lord in heaven, the world is wide and wonderful from way up there. And then, after we landed again, Skinny and I talked some more. And what do you know? We were all three of us kind of hungry by then. So Tate drove us over to the ranch house and Miranda cooked us a big meal. Then after we ate, we drove Skinny back to the airfield.''

''And somewhere during all that, you found yourself a job?''

Granny fluttered her artfully mascaraed lashes. ''See, honey pie, seems Skinny's been looking for a receptionist and secretary. You know, an all-around multitaskin' girl Friday type, to help out at the airfield, give the place a little touch of class, if you know where I'm heading here.''

Molly set down the remote. ''You're hiring on as Skinny Jordan's secretary out at Wide Skies airfield?''

Granny gave Molly's arm an affectionate slap. ''Don't give me that doubtful look. I know how to answer a phone. And I can type, too—as long as no one asks me to be in a big hurry about it.'' She sent a thumb over her shoulder in the direction of the computer in the corner. ''And who was it that figured out how to print four-by-six pictures when you got that new digital camera last Christmas?''

Molly looked at Granny sideways. ''You know you don't *have* to work.'' After the accident at the iron-works, Granny got disability for a while. Then there was some unemployment insurance. But that had long ago run out. She had a dinky retirement pension that kept her in pocket change. ''There's plenty with what I bring in from the shop,'' Molly said. ''And in a year, you'll be eligible for Social Security.''

Granny waved a hand. ''It's not about the money, dearie mine. It's truly not. This is about dreams. *My* dreams, coming true.''

Dreams, Molly thought, and realized that kind of settled it. She asked, softly, ''What kind of hours will you be working?''

''Nothing too challenging, I promise you. Three, maybe four hours a day—and I'm not to the best part of all yet…''

''Which is?''

''Skinny'll pay me fifty dollars a week in cash— more than enough for gas to get out there. The rest'll go for flight lessons.''

''Skinny Jordan is going to—''

''That's right, june bug. Skinny has promised to teach me to fly. Won't be long, dear one. Your granny is going to be a licensed pilot. You just wait and see.''

Over the week that followed Granny woke in the morning smiling. She hummed Bob Wills tunes as she fixed breakfast. She was back at home by the time Molly returned from the Cut. She smiled all through dinner and chattered away about what had happened out at Wide Skies that day, especially whatever she'd learned in her lesson from Skinny.

Not once the whole week did Granny ask for her shotgun.

Molly found this new, lighthearted, grinning granny a little disorienting. All Molly's life, she'd listened to Granny grumble about men and declare that the lot of them ought to be floated out to sea in a boat with a hole in it, that except for a sperm injection now and then, what was a man good for but heartache, anyway?

Now Granny hummed as she went around the house, and she talked about Skinny and *oohed* and *ahhed* over the presents that Tate kept on sending her. No single discouraging word about men crossed her thin lips. She looked younger, too. A decade, at least. She kept her chin a little higher and her back a little straighter.

Molly knew she would get used to her new, happier, man-friendly granny eventually. That wasn't the problem. Not really.

The real problem was Tate.

The problem was how she couldn't stop wondering why, after she'd told him she wouldn't see him any more, after she'd made it so painfully clear that she would never, under any circumstances, become Mrs. Bravo; why, when she refused to do what he wanted her to do…

Why had he still gone right ahead and taken her granny for a ride in his plane? Why had he set it up so Granny could realize her dream of flying a plane herself someday? Why did he keep on sending Granny gifts?

And then there was the diner where Dixie worked. Molly's customers told her that Tate was still having his breakfast there, still sitting next to Ray at the counter, still chatting up Dixie when she poured his coffee and brought him his food.

It didn't add up. It was not the least bit like him, to be so kind and friendly and gracious when he wasn't getting what he wanted.

And then there was his manner with Molly herself. He'd treated her civilly when he came to pick up Granny on Sunday—yeah, there had been that long, slow once-over. But even that had been friendly enough. Not once had he indulged in a single sneer or a dirty look. And when Molly passed him on Center Street Wednesday, he said, real pleasantly, "How you doing, Molly?" And with a nod and a quick smile, he walked on by.

Tate Bravo had not done one bitter, hard-hearted or overbearing thing since Molly had told him she wouldn't go out with him again and he'd better stay away. And that was downright strange. Worse than strange. It was…scary. Molly found the new pleasant and reasonable Tate Bravo harder to accept than her suddenly employed, man-friendly granny.

She found it harder because it really did get to her. It made her soften toward him. Made her start thinking that maybe—just maybe—there might be a chance for the two of them as a couple.

Which was crazy, insane and absolutely impossible.

Wasn't it?

On Thursday, Donetta Brewer came shoving through the door of the Cut. Since she'd had her acrylic nails filed the day before, a cut just two weeks ago and her color touched up last Friday, Molly knew right away this visit had nothing to do with any pressing beauty needs. Donetta helped herself to a cup of cold sweet tea and plunked down in a red chair. She didn't even bother to pick up a magazine.

"Y'all won't believe it." Her eyes had a rabid kind of gleam to them.

"Oh, Donetta, what?" asked one of the other stylists much too eagerly, as far as Molly was concerned.

"Ray Deekins has just gone and got himself hired by Davey Luster over at Junction Hardware."

Everyone gasped—and then giggled. "No."

"You are kidding."

"Y'all can't be serious."

"As a bad perm," announced Donetta. "And that's not the best of it. The best is, Tate *made* Davey hire Ray."

"Well, how did he do that?" asked Sharon, the nail technician.

Somebody giggled and Donetta turned to Sharon wearing a superior and knowing look. "Honey, you need yourself a crash course in the way things work in this town. Tate—and technically his brother Tucker, too, though Tucker hardly matters as he's long gone—is partners with Davey in the hardware store. Just like he's partners with Russ Johnson at the grocery store and Morley Pribble at the Gas 'n Go— and also with just about every other businessman in this town. If Tate Bravo says to hire someone, that someone gets hired. However…" She let that one word trail off deliciously.

The others were leaning forward, eyes gleaming every bit as rabidly as Donetta's.

"What?"

"Tell us."

"Donetta. Come *on*."

"Stop *torturing* us."

Donetta drew it out by indulging in one more sip of tea, the ice cubes rattling in her tall, sweating glass. After about a decade and a half, she swallowed. "Word is—and I have it from the best authority— Tate also told Davey he could take Ray's wages from the Bravo boys' share." Another gasp went up from the assembled women. Donetta turned then and looked straight at Molly. "I gotta hand it to you, girl. That man wants you and he wants you bad. I never thought I'd see the day that Tate Bravo would volunteer to have anyone's wages taken out of *his* share—let alone the wages of Ray Deekins, who is a very sweet man, but about as useless in the working world as a milk bucket under a bull."

Chapter Nine

Molly couldn't help being touched and impressed by Tate's ongoing efforts to get along with the people she cared about. And not only to get along with them, but to make their lives better, to hold out a hand and give them a chance to live their dreams.

Well, okay. In Ray's case, maybe a job wasn't exactly his dream. But he had been trying to get up the nerve and energy to go job-hunting again. Now, he wouldn't have to. Thanks to Tate, he was employed. Maybe, being motivated by his desire to help Dixie bring home the bacon, he would even hold on to this job. It was long shot, but you never could tell.

Then, on Saturday after work, Molly went over to Dixie's double-wide to try on the maid-of-honor dress that Dixie had chosen for her.

* * *

Dixie and Ray were sitting at Dixie's prized retro chrome-skirted table making pink crepe-paper flowers when Molly came in the door.

Ray looked up and smiled and went back to twisting crepe paper. Dixie said, "Hey, baby." She held up a swatch of crepe paper and a section of thin wire. "We're making three thousand of these. Whew. What a job." Under the table sat a row of open boxes with more paper flowers spilling out. Dixie's ancient long-haired white cat, Snowflake, who was blind in one eye and not as spry as she used to be, had got hold of one. She was listlessly batting it around on the speckled linoleum. "Gonna staple them to a white trellis." She sent Ray an adoring smile. "Our wedding arch."

"I'll be glad to help," Molly offered.

"Nope," answered Ray proudly. "We been working on these suckers for weeks and we have passed the two-thousand-five-hundred mark. This is the home stretch you're seeing here."

"Your dress is on the bed, baby." Dixie gestured toward the dark-paneled narrow hallway and her and Ray's bedroom at the end of it. "Try it on. Let us see…"

Obediently Molly went to the bedroom and found a frothing mound of lavender and lace spilling across the bed. There was even a wide-brimmed hat decorated with purple and white silk roses and dripping ribbons down the back. With a sigh, Molly put the thing on—hat and lavender fifties-style sandals included.

When Molly emerged from the bedroom, hands pressed low to keep her skirt from scraping the narrow walls, Dixie dropped the crepe-paper flower she was working on and sniffed back the tears that swam in her eyes. "Oh, baby. You are just beautiful."

"Yeah," Ray agreed, looking excessively solemn. "Yeah, you are."

Molly caught her big hat before it slid off her head. "I need a hat pin, I guess. And maybe, when this is over, I'll just move to Atlanta."

"Beautiful," Dixie announced for the second time. "Like I always say, it is amazing the treasures you can find at Vanna's Vintage Vibe. I was thinking you'd need a tuck or two at the waist. But no, it's just perfect, after all."

Being pregnant did have its advantages. Molly took off the monstrous hat and set it on the chartreuse Danish modern sofa a few feet from the table where Dixie and Ray sat. "I haven't seen *your* dress yet."

Dixie shook her head. "I had Vanna hold on to it for me. Ray might sneak in the closet and have a peek if I kept it here." Ray gave her a look that clearly said he was not a man to go stealing peeks at women's dresses. "I'll tell you this much," Dixie volunteered coyly. "Mine's pink and the skirt is even wider than yours, which is why we need a big arch and lots of flowers to cover it." She beamed another of those googly-eyed smiles at Ray and recited, "'Married in pink, of you he'll forever think.' Isn't that right, Ray honey?"

Ray made a low, slightly embarrassed sound of agreement and busily twisted wire over a wad of crepe paper.

Dixie stared at the top of his head, still with that long-gone look of love in her eyes. "And Ray is wearing a powder-blue tux with a black string tie and ruffles all down his shirtfront.'' Ray gave a slightly pained but resigned shrug.

''And baby?'' Dixie tore her gaze away from the top of Ray's head and looked at Molly again. ''I hope this isn't going to upset you too awful much, given as how I know that you and Tate have, er, parted ways, so to speak....''

Molly felt kind of faint suddenly—and also compelled to clarify, ''Since we were never together, you can't really say that we've parted ways.''

''Now, baby, don't get testy. Please.''

''I am not testy, I'm only making things perfectly clear.''

Dixie sighed. ''All right, then. You were never together. Now, is it okay with you if I finish what I started to say?''

Ray had looked up. He, along with Dixie, was watching Molly warily. Even Snowflake had given up toying with her crepe-paper flower and sat on her haunches, staring at Molly through her one good eye. Molly knew what was coming—she just couldn't quite believe it. Thankfully that moment of nausea seemed to have passed. She indulged in a shrug. ''Sure. Go ahead.''

''Well, even if you're not on good terms with Tate right now—''

''I wouldn't say I'm exactly on *bad* terms with Tate.''

Dixie's lush lips pursed up. ''Baby, will you just let me finish?'' Molly nodded, her mouth shut. And Dixie delivered the big news at last. ''Whatever you think about Tate, *we* like him. A lot. And he has just helped Ray to get a job—and he's been real nice to your granny, by the way. So Ray asked him to be Ray's best man. Tate has agreed.''

Tate had agreed to be Ray's best man. Whoever would have imagined it? Molly felt positively giddy, for some crazy reason. A giggle rose up in her throat. She put her hand over her mouth to keep from bursting into a laugh.

''Is something funny?'' Dixie asked, getting irritated.

The giggle subdued, Molly took her hand away from her mouth. ''Oh, no. Not a thing. I think Tate being Ray's best man is a great idea.''

Ray and Dixie turned their heads in unison and stared, wearing matching expressions of shocked amazement. Under the table, Snowflake squinted at Molly as if she didn't believe a word of it. Dixie said, plainly doubtful, ''You do?''

Molly nodded, with firmness. And then she couldn't help asking, ''Will Tate be wearing a powder-blue tux with a ruffled shirt, too?''

''Not as many ruffles as mine,'' muttered Ray, a wistful light in his eye.

''But that's a yes on the light-blue tux?''

Both Ray and Dixie nodded. A warm-fuzzy, sentimental sensation moved through Molly. It was so sweet, really, Ray and Dixie all worried about how she was going to take the idea of Tate being Ray's best man.

''I understand,'' she reassured them again. ''I know he's been good to you—and to Granny, too. I really do think it's a fine idea.''

And besides, she wouldn't feel quite so over-the-top in her lavender ruffles and big picture hat if Tate was there beside her all dressed up in a powder-blue tux.

The day before the wedding was town council-meeting day.

The meeting room off the library was packed, with folks standing in back, spilling into the hallway. Nobody wanted to miss the show when Mayor Molly O'Dare and Councilman Tate Bravo locked horns again. Just about every person in town who wasn't a total recluse or under the age of three knew by then that Molly was pregnant with Tate's child. They also knew that in spite of his persistent and creative efforts to convince her otherwise, she had refused to take his hand in marriage.

The minutes of the previous meeting and the town financial reports were read by the clerk and treasurer respectively. A few minor issues came first on the agenda, giving time for building anticipation over the yelling and angry words that would start flying when they got on the issues of allocating funds for Center Street improvements proposed by Councilman Bravo, and Mayor O'Dare's plan for community-supported indigent and shut-in care.

The indigent and shut-in care issue came up first of the two. The townsfolk held their collective breaths as Mayor Molly announced the issue. The mayor introduced the committee head, Estella Lopez, who spoke for a few minutes, outlining the plan as she had in the previous meeting, explaining the changes made in the meantime and adding new information and developments.

There was discussion. Very calm and reasonable

discussion. Discussion that didn't include Councilman Bravo, who sat silent and scarily pleasant-faced through not only the council's discussion of the issue, but also the hour or so when citizens were allowed to step forward and speak their opinions for or against, and the question-and-answer period that followed.

At the end, Tate Bravo finally spoke up.

Everyone knew the fireworks were coming.

But he only made two specific suggestions for reining in the expense of the program and asked that the budget for it should be cut by a third. "Is that possible, do you think, Mayor O'Dare?"

The mayor, with a slight flush on her cheeks and surprise in her eyes, turned to her committee head. Estella said cutting the budget by a third was impossible. However, just maybe, with a heavier volunteer emphasis and some matching funds, they could manage to cut the expense to the town coffers by a fourth. "I'll get the committee working on it right away."

"Do that," said Tate. "And I'm sure that next month we can get the ball rolling."

There was dead silence. Not one person in that room could believe his own ears. Tate Bravo had just as good as given the go-ahead to a program that wouldn't make money for anyone.

The Center Street Improvement Project came next. Citizens licked their lips. Surely the expected fireworks would start exploding then.

Councilman Bravo introduced *his* committee head and the same process occurred as with Mayor Molly's plan—including the reasonable discourse and the pleasant give-and-take all around.

In the end, it was the mayor, with a soft smile for

Tate Bravo, announcing that now they were moving along on the indigent care plan, they needed to make sure that the tax base stayed strong. Better access to Center Street businesses should increase spending, which meant more sales tax collected to replenish the town coffers.

She suggested a few cuts in the plan's basic budget. The cuts were accepted. The council voted. The plan passed.

Dazed and amazed, the good citizens of Tate's Junction poured out of the meeting hall into the hot Texas sunshine. Not one of them could believe what they had just witnessed. Mayor Molly and Councilman Bravo had spent four hours working *together* for the good of the town.

Molly's mother got married at two the next afternoon, out in Patriot Park, beneath an arch of three thousand pink crepe-paper flowers. Dixie's dress was the color of Pepto-Bismol. Tight on top, showing off Dixie's magnificent cleavage and still-slender waist, the dress had fat puff sleeves and a wide full-length beruffled Hostess Snowball of a skirt. Her pink veil sprouted from the back of her head, poufed on top and trailed down behind her to float above her ruffled pink train.

Ray, in his sky-blue tux with the explosion of ruffles in front, looked a little like an aging refugee from some seventies senior prom.

But they did look happy, the two of them. They stood under the pink arch and said their vows out loud and proud and Pastor Partridge from the local Church of the Way of Our Lord pronounced them husband and wife.

When Ray kissed his bride, Molly found herself looking past the embracing newlyweds to the other man in a blue tux—the man who stood up beside Ray. Tate looked right back at her, a steady, knowing kind of look.

Her insides went all hot and mushy, and she smiled—feeling ridiculously hopeful, weak in the knees and glad to be so. She supposed the relentless kindness he'd kept on displaying in the face of her every insistent refusal had finally worn her down.

And oh, it did feel good. To admit she intended to give Tate Bravo—and whatever kind of life she might have at his side—at least the beginnings of a chance. Tate smiled back at her, that slow smile of his, the one that made her body feel shimmery and hungry for his touch, the one that made her heart go light as a white, fluffy cloud in a limitless blue Texas sky.

The four-piece band—old friends of Ray's—struck up a rousing rendition of "Love Will Keep Us Together." The bride and groom led the way down the makeshift aisle, which was really only a space on the grass between two clumps of standing spectators. Tate and Molly followed, also side by side.

And they stayed that way—side by side—for the rest of the day, as they joined in the Tate's Junction Independence Day festivities. By three, Tate had shed his tux jacket and his tie. He'd rolled up his sleeves and loosened the top two buttons of his ruffled shirt. It was ninety-six degrees in the shade, no scorcher by Texas standards, but hot enough to make a man want to rid himself of some of his clothes.

Molly ditched her picture hat. She gave it to Granny, who was looking sharp in a light cotton shirt and her favorite wide-legged pants and walking around with her arm through Skinny Jordan's.

My, my. Love—or at least more cordial relations between the O'Dare women and certain members of the male gender—seemed to be the order of the day.

Tate played horseshoes and won. They had hot dogs and Cokes from the 4H booth and watched the parade that marched down Center Street at four. At six, it would be Molly's turn in the Dunk the Politician booth, so at five-thirty, she told Tate she had to run home and change.

"I'll go with you…" The light in his eyes had her thinking naughty thoughts about how much could be accomplished between a forceful man and an eager woman in just a few moments in a quiet, empty house.

She spotted Granny over by the Knights of Columbus booth, with Skinny. "Come on." She grabbed Tate's hand. "Let me get my hat from Granny and we can go."

"Have a seat," she said, sending her hat sailing toward the sofa as she led him in her front door. "There's cold tea in the fridge if you want some. I'll just…" But by then he'd caught her hand and hauled her to him. "Tate," she said chidingly, a slight smile on her lips that she knew would just egg him on. He wrapped his arm around her waist, gathering her in close. He looked into her eyes, and she sighed and reminded him, "We've only got a few minutes…"

He chuckled then. The sound vibrated against her

breasts and it was lovely, oh it really was: just the two of them stealing an intimate moment or two, in the cool dimness of her little house. In the other room, the window air conditioner hummed, and Molly shivered in delight.

"Cold?" he asked.

"Not in the least." She wrapped her arms around his neck.

He lowered his mouth and she raised hers.

They kissed, and it was a kiss of promise. Of sweet possibilities. She eased her lips apart, welcoming the tender invasion of his tongue, sucking on it, then following it back where it came from with her own.

She felt the cool air against her back as one by one he released the tiny row of hooks there. Oh, that Tate. So good with his hands. And so helpful. After all, she did need to get out of her big, lavender maid-of-honor dress.

Those hands went roaming. He stroked her bare back, his fingers nimble and knowing. In one easy flick, he had her bra undone.

"Oh!" she exclaimed, breaking the deep kiss and pulling back to look up at him through eyes much too heavy to open all the way. "I don't need my bra unhooked, thank you," she told him in a lazy drawl.

"But I do." His head swooped down and he claimed her mouth again in a kiss that heated her body and melted her heart. Oh, she could have stood there kissing him forever.

But in ten minutes flat she had to be back at that booth and ready for dunking. She squirmed away, pressing on his hard, hot chest, craning her head back.

''Tate. I have to—'' She giggled as he captured her lips all over again.

And she let him kiss her some more—well, okay, she more than *let* him. She moaned into his mouth and pressed her breasts to his chest and lifted her hips so she could rub against the hard ridge in his trousers that said he really, really wanted to get her prone with all her clothes off.

He was pulling her balloon lace sleeves down over her arms when she finally had to admit that if they went any further, she wouldn't make it to the dunking booth at all that afternoon.

She broke their kiss for the third time, squirming around so her back was to him. He still held on tight, his arms wrapped good and hard around her, but at least now, unless she craned her head back, he couldn't capture her mouth. She intended to exert every ounce of willpower she possessed to keep from doing that.

He slid the eyelet sleeves down her arms and was kissing her neck, his hands on the move again. He pushed the front of her half-pulled-down dress out of his way and slid those hands up under her unhooked bra.

''Tate.'' She said the word on a hungry groan as his hands cupped her breasts and squeezed.

''Um?'' He opened his mouth and sucked on her neck.

''Tate…'' She pushed her bottom back against him and moaned. ''You are an octopus…''

''Is that a complaint, Madame Mayor?'' He nibbled on her ear.

''Well…'' She lost her train of thought as he

started tugging on her nipples. "Oh! Really, I... um..." Words deserted her—and she knew they would stay gone until he stopped touching her.

She grabbed both his hands and peeled them away. He didn't fight it—well, at least not too hard. He brushed one more kiss against the side of her neck and reluctantly let her go. She grabbed the front of her dress and faced him, backing toward the hallway and her room.

He laughed then, a rough, deep laugh that sang along her nerves and hollowed her out down below. "Hurry up," he advised. "You don't want to be late to get a few good, hard dunkings." She turned for the bedroom. And he said, "Molly."

She stopped and they looked at each other for a breath-held kind of moment. "What?"

"It's been too damn long."

"Yeah," she admitted with no hesitation. "Yeah, Tate. It has."

They made it to the dunking booth a few minutes late. But no one seemed to care all that much. Molly, in a T-shirt that said Ms. Mayor To You and a pair of short shorts, got up on the platform above the thousand-gallon tank of water. Everyone seemed to want a shot at her. If it hadn't been for such a good cause, she could have been insulted.

She got dunked more times than the town treasurer or the two councilmen or the three county supervisors who'd volunteered earlier, grinning and waving every time she dropped into the cool water. The proceeds were going for books and supplies for district schools—and besides, it just plain felt good to be out of her big dress and to be soaking wet on a hot summer evening.

When her turn in the dunking booth was over, she darted into the tent in back and changed into the fresh pair of shorts and a dry tank top she'd brought with her.

As the night came on, she and Tate danced together in the grass to a local country band. They had barbecue from the DAR booth. And after full dark, they watched the fireworks display together, sitting on the grass with all the other folks, making sounds of awe and wonder as the bright colored lights exploded in the wide night sky.

They were walking toward Tate's Cadillac when Molly spotted Granny and Skinny not far away. She waved and Granny waved back.

"You have a fine night, now," Granny said, and the light in her eyes said she'd have a fine night, too. Skinny had his arm draped easily across her shoulders.

Who would ever have thought it? The man-hatingest woman in Throckleford County, with a romantic gleam in her eyes and Skinny Jordan close at her side.

Her fingers twined with Tate's, Molly climbed the wide steps to the ranch house's long front porch. At the front door, Tate paused to punch in an alarm code. They went in, and she waited beside him on the polished Texas pink granite of the entryway floor as he punched more buttons to reset the alarm.

Then he turned to her. He backed her up against the wall by the doors to his study, right next to one of his mother's bad paintings—this one of a bow-legged cowhand leaning on a rail fence. Bracing a hand to either side of her head, he leaned forward just enough to tease her with a brushing kiss.

She gave a slow look to one and then the other of his imprisoning arms. "I do believe you have trapped me."

He lifted a dark brow. "But are you *willing* to be trapped?"

She thought about that, lazily slipping her foot from its sandal and hooking one powder-blue trouser cuff with her big toe. "Yes," she admitted as she ran her toe lightly along the hair-rough inside of his leg. "You have me now and I am willing...."

His mouth met hers. The kiss was long and wet and sweet, punctuated by sighs and low, eager moans. Molly's knees went deliciously weak and she made full use of the supporting wall at her back.

When they came up for air, Tate's housekeeper was standing near the foot of the wide staircase, looking as if she'd been just about to duck for cover when they spotted her.

Molly stiffened her passion-wobbly knees and pushed herself away from the wall, turning in Tate's arms so she faced the housekeeper. "Hey, Miranda." She put on a big, cheerful smile and hoped her cheeks weren't as flame-red as they felt. "How've you been?"

Miranda dipped her dark head. "Just fine, Mayor Molly." She said each word with care. "Nice to see you again."

One arm still wrapped good and tight around Molly, Tate nodded at the housekeeper. "I'm okay for the night. Go ahead and take off. See you in the morning."

Miranda muttered a soft, *"Buenos noches,"* and fled toward the kitchen.

Molly waited till she was gone to remark, "I think we've embarrassed poor Miranda by our shocking behavior right here in the front hall."

He shrugged. "I'm the boss." And he drew her around to face him again, gathering her tight in both arms, lowering his head to nibble her ear. He whispered between nibbles, "I can be as shocking as I want to be."

Molly moaned, then stiffened a little. "Shame on you." She lightly punched his shoulder. "Miranda's a good Catholic woman. She probably knows what kinds of outrageous things you intend to do to me as soon as you get me into your bedroom."

"Probably?" He laughed his wonderfully deep, rough laugh and then, yanking her close again, he caught her earlobe, so lightly, between his teeth and flicked it with his tongue.

Her blood humming hotly in her ears, Molly whispered, "Little does Miranda know you won't be the only one doing shocking things tonight…"

He licked the side of her neck. "Go ahead. Drive me crazy."

She grabbed the open front of his rumpled tux shirt in either fist and got right up in his face. "Oh, you watch. I definitely will."

He craned back enough to grin down at her, his eyes lazy-lidded and his mouth temptingly soft from kissing her. She let go of his shirt and pushed away from him, the movement so quick, he lost his hold on her.

"Hey…" He tried to grab her again.

But she only laughed and reached for the hem of her tank top, holding his hot gaze as she slowly, teasingly began sliding it upward over her rib cage.

"Wait." His eyes gleamed dark as night.

"Wait?" She let go of the half-raised tank top to step in close to him again. "Are you crazy?" Surging up on tiptoe, she planted a quick, hard kiss on his mouth.

"Crazy?" He frowned—and then he grinned. "No doubt about it. But there's something I…" He didn't finish. He had the funniest nervous kind of look on his face.

What was going on here? Tate Bravo at a loss for words? This couldn't be happening. She lifted up again and pressed another short, hard kiss on his lips. "What? Tell me. Don't be shy." She giggled and rolled her eyes. Yeah, right. Tate Bravo. Shy.

But then she peered closer. Why, he actually did look kind of bashful. About what?

He grabbed her hand. "Come on," he commanded gruffly, turning on his heel and setting off. Fast.

"Tate…" She hung back, trying to toe up her sandal and slide it back on before he dragged her away from it.

But he gave her no chance for that. "This way." He kept going, his strong jaw set, his expression intent, hauling her along behind.

It did appear he was heading toward the master bedroom in back. So then no problem, she thought. She stopped objecting and kicked off her other sandal.

Willingly she let him tow her, barefooted, to where she very much wanted to go.

In his bedroom, he swung the door shut, flicked on a light, and led her to the big, heavily carved bureau against a nearby wall. He let go of her hand long enough to slide open the top drawer and take out a black velvet ring box.

By then, she knew what was coming.

He dropped to one knee on the thickly padded antique rug and she looked down at his upturned, handsome face—and tried to stop him. "Tate. Listen, I…"

But he'd already flipped open the little box, revealing a diamond that put Lena Lou Billingsworth's paltry four carats to shame. "Marry me, Molly." He was smiling, an open, glorious kind of smile. "Marry me and let's give our baby his daddy's name. Marry me. Be my wife." He chuckled. "Make it so that Miranda will never again have to be embarrassed when she catches us kissing out in the hallway." He took out the ring and dropped the box to the rug.

A big, fat *yes* almost got out of her mouth. But somehow, she stopped it. She slid her left hand behind her back where he couldn't get to it and she told him, with deepest regret, "No, Tate. I can't do that. I really can't. Not yet."

Chapter Ten

From his completely unaccustomed position on his knees, Tate gaped up at Molly in stunned disbelief.

Her silky gold hair, which had dried coiled and curly after all the dunking that afternoon, fell forward around her flushed face. Her lips, still soft and red from his kisses, trembled. Her golden-brown eyes pleaded with him, filled with regret.

Regret?

What in hell for? She didn't need to regret a damn thing. She only needed to open that plump, tempting mouth of hers and say *yes*. She only had to hold out her hand, accept his ring on her finger and come into his arms, all his at last.

But she was doing none of those things. Oh, no, not Molly.

Molly was *again* telling him no.

Numb disbelief began to melt into hot rage. He blinked and looked down at himself.

On his *knees* in front of her. Could he sink any lower?

How did this keep happening to him? Where she was concerned, he always came off feeling chuckle-headed as a damn prairie dog.

Why just look at all he'd done to claim her. The daily presents for Dusty—a lot of them damned difficult to get, you'd better believe. And not only presents. Oh, no. Because of him, Dusty was learning to fly. And what about how he'd gotten her that job at Skinny's airfield—not to mention the very personal attention of Skinny himself.

And then there was Dixie. How about the way he'd kissed up to *her?* Eating at the diner five days a week, lapping up the flapjacks and sausage, the biscuits and gravy. His arteries were probably hard as rocks by now. He could be headed straight for a coronary, could have sacrificed his health, just for the chance to cozy up to Molly's mother and get to know Ray.

And speaking of Ray…

Hadn't Tate gone against his own principles, pulling strings with Davey Luster, forcing him to hire Ray?

And then there was that town council meeting yesterday. Hadn't he eaten crow and pretended to like it, sitting there, grinning like a long-gone fool while they kicked around Molly's bleeding-heart plan for indigent care? Hadn't he spoken right up at the end, gracious as some old maid at high tea, asking for a few more cuts in the plan and then promising it would get his vote?

And all for what?

To end up on his knees being told no.

He swept to his feet and glared down at her. "Damn you, Molly."

"Oh, Tate..." She shrank back.

He opened his mouth to start shouting at her. She needed a good, hard shake or two.

Oh, yeah, he was going to give it to her right and proper. Let her know just what he thought of her, after all his sucking up to her crazy family, after giving the go-ahead to dip into town coffers for a program that wouldn't make a red cent for anyone....

But then, in that split second before he ripped her a new one, some small, cautious voice in the back of his head reminded him softly that he ought to be honest—at least with himself.

Now think about it, Tate. Do you really feel that put upon for all you did to get your chance with her?

He blinked and looked—*really* looked—at the woman in front of him. She had fallen back another step. Her gaze was locked on his face, her expression worried and watchful and a little bit scared of him. In a minute, she would be whirling, slamming out the door.

And he had to admit it. Even if she wouldn't marry him, even if he never found a way to convince her of the absolute necessity of giving their kid his daddy's name. Even if she never became his wife...

He wanted her for as long as he could have her.

He sure as hell *didn't* want her to leave him tonight.

And that's not all, is it? that small voice in his head was asking.

No. No, it wasn't.

He might as well get straight about this in his own mind. The plain fact was, he had actually *enjoyed* pleasing Dusty. There had been a real sense of accomplishment in being the one who turned Molly's granny from a man-hating crone with a shotgun in her hands to a handsome old woman with her head held high and a welcoming smile on her wrinkled lips. He was glad he'd been able to help her find work— and he was downright pleased with himself that he'd gotten her hooked up with sweet old Skinny Jordan.

As to Dixie and Ray...

The bald truth was, he *liked* taking his breakfast at the diner, having a little company during what had always seemed to him a lonely meal. And he'd be a lying dog if he didn't admit he was *proud* that he'd reached out a hand, man-to-man, to help Ray. And hadn't he been deeply touched when Ray stuttered out a request that he be Ray's best man?

And what about that damned proposal for indigent and shut-in care? Looking back, he had to admit he'd felt a tightness of self-satisfaction in his chest when he'd looked into to the eyes of the Tate's Junction citizenry and declared himself willing to support a plan for the public good and the public good alone.

"Tate?" She was still looking worried, but at least she'd stopped backing up. He realized he'd balled his right hand to a fist. The big diamond was slicing into his palm. He lifted it, palm up, and opened his fingers to reveal the rim of red around the sharp-edged stone. "Oh, Tate," she cried. "You went and hurt yourself..." She moved up close, all feminine and flustered at the very idea that he might be injured. She reached for his hand.

And he let her take it, heat bursting through him just at her lightest touch. "It's nothing," he growled. "A dinky little scratch."

She did the most confounding thing then. She plucked the diamond out of his hand, spread his fingers wide open and pressed her lips to the tiny cut. She raised her head, her amber gaze seeking and finding his.

Their eyes met—and something exploded inside him. Something hot and full of light and wonder. Something that burned and healed at the same time.

"You've got blood on your mouth," he heard himself whispering.

And she rose on tiptoe and pressed her lips to his. He kissed her—gently, carefully, a kiss of deep yearning, yet with considerable restraint.

When she pulled back, the blood on her lips was gone. In his own mouth he tasted a fading hint of copper.

"Please, Tate. Try to understand. I grew up not even knowing who my father was, listening to Granny tell me over and over that there was nothing so bad or so dangerous as the human male, seeing my poor mama get used and abused by one useless, violent, no-good man after another. Even if you were as sweet and easygoing as Ray Deekins, you'd still be taking on a big challenge to try to get me to marry you, to convince me to give my trust over to you in such a deep and important way." She looked down at his hand, still held in hers, and petted the scratch on his

palm, which had already given up its few drops of
blood and remained nothing more than a thin red line.

"And, Tate?" She slanted an upward glance at
him.

He resisted the urge to grab her and grind his
mouth down on hers. *No,* he thought. *Let her finish.*
He forced out a low noise, trying to sound encouraging, holding his hand very still where it lay cupped
in her smaller one.

Apparently she *was* encouraged. She continued,
"Well, no offense, but you are not, as a rule, a sweet
and easygoing man. You like to be the boss and you
like things done your way—and I'm not calling you
down for that. I'm not all that sweet myself, and I
like to do things *my* way."

He grunted. "Tell me about."

She made a wry kind of face and then got all serious and eager again. "In the past few weeks, you
have truly amazed me." Well. He did like the sound
of that. "All the wonderful things you've been doing
for my family, how really calm and patient you've
been with me and my refusal to do what you want
me to do." As she spoke, his heart seemed to get a
little bigger inside his chest. His blood raced faster
and the glow that had started inside him grew all the
brighter. She continued, "You are..." She struggled
to find words.

He longed to help her out, to provide a few helpful
adjectives that might begin to describe how heroic
and noble he'd been. But, no, she had a right to come
up with her own words of praise and admiration.

Somehow he managed to keep his mouth shut.

And eventually, she went on, "You have me starting to think that maybe it *could* work out between us, in the end. That we could make a real marriage..." She frowned, looking puzzled, "Whatever that is."

He wasn't all that sure what a good marriage was himself. But he wasn't about to let her know that. He said with great intensity and determination, "We can, Molly. I know we can."

A sad little smile kind of flirted with the corners of her mouth. Gently, she put the engagement ring back in his hand. Tenderly she folded his fingers around it. "Oh, Tate. How could you know that? You've got no more clue than I do what a good marriage is."

It was exactly what he'd been thinking a moment before. But still, it irked him to hear her say it out loud.

She turned from him and padded over to his bed, dropping to the studded leather bench at the foot of it. "And when have *I* ever seen a good marriage close up? That's a big, fat *never*. I have no idea how to be a good wife. And I'm sorry to say it, with you being so wonderful and all lately, but I still have my doubts that you're husband material." She flung out a hand in his general direction. "I mean, look at you, Tate." She shook her head.

Reasonably certain he wouldn't be too thrilled with whatever she was going to say next, he looked down at his half-unbuttoned, rumpled tux shirt and sissified sky-blue slacks. When he met her eyes again, he shrugged and tried to make light of whatever criticism seemed to be coming his way. "This getup's pretty bad, I'll admit. But don't blame me. It was your mother and her groom who chose it."

She gave him one of those table-clearing gusty sighs of hers. ''Oh, Tate.''

He shook his head. ''You know, I'm not so sure I like it when you start in with the 'Oh, Tates.' ''

''It's just that, well, you were raised by Ol' Tuck. And there is no one more hardheaded and overbearing than he was. And then, look at your grandmother…''

His grandmother had been a woman of impeccable taste and breeding. Gruffly he demanded. ''What was wrong with her?''

''Oh, you know…''

''She was a fine woman.''

''I'm not saying she wasn't. It's only, well, the hoity-toity family background and all that. Wasn't she from Savannah or something?''

''Charleston, as a matter of fact.''

''Savannah. Charleston. Whatever. A great beauty in her time, isn't that right?''

He answered proudly, ''Yes, she was.''

''All the spunk and vinegar bred right out of her.''

He frowned. ''Well, now. I wouldn't say—''

''Oh, Tate. You know it's true. Your grandmother was so well-bred and retiring, she'd only ask sweetly, 'How high?' when Ol' Tuck said, 'Jump.' And then, what about your poor mama?''

''What about her?'' Tate growled.

''Oh, well. You know…''

''If I did, Molly,'' he said carefully, ''I wouldn't have asked.''

''Well, ahem, I mean, was there ever a woman so pitiful and beaten down as that?'' He would have answered in his mother's defense, but she gave him no chance. ''Uh-uh. Your granddaddy ruled her just the way he ruled your grandma. You have to face it. You were born, bred and raised to believe that women aren't as good as men, that a woman's place is in the home, flat on her back, with her mouth shut. In the world where you grew up, women fluttered around arranging flowers and looking decorative and never daring to argue with the master of the house." So what's wrong with that? he longed to ask—but had sense enough not to. Though his mother was a little too jumpy and withdrawn for his taste, he'd always thought of his grandmother as the perfect example of what a well-bred woman ought to be. Quiet. Soft-spoken. Not to mention obedient. Molly capped the long list of insults to his family with, "You've never seen a real marriage close up any more than I have."

"A *real* marriage?" he huffed. "Listen here, Molly. My grandfather and grandmother *were* married. My mother was married to my father. Those were *real* marriages, don't try to tell me they weren't."

Now Molly wore an irksome patient look. "Tate, you know what I mean. I'm not talking about a preacher saying the right words or a piece of paper that declares you husband and wife. I'm talking about in *here*." She fisted her hand and thumped herself in the chest with it. "I'm talking about give and take, about a man and a woman working together as equals to make a better life for themselves—and for their babies."

He gestured broadly. "Look around. Life's pretty good here as it is."

She shook her head. "There you go talking about

all your money. Well, I don't only mean money. There *are* other things that matter, you know.''

"Golly, Molly," he muttered, heavy on the irony. "Thanks for pointing that out. I had no idea."

She looked pained. "Can you not be sarcastic? Please?"

Terrific. He was in for it now. She'd give it to him in detail, what a money-grubbing SOB he was.

But she surprised him. She said nothing more—only looked at him, eyes wide and mouth grimly shut.

"So, then." He gave her a long, slow once-over, sneering while he did it. "What are you doing here, if there's no damn hope for us?"

She hiked up her chin and pulled back her shoulders, sitting tall and proud. "I didn't say there wasn't any hope."

"Could have fooled me."

"I was only trying to get you to see what we're up against, that's all." She rose then from the leather bench and approached him—cautiously. He watched her coming, holding her gaze, keeping his own eyes steady and narrowed. She got right up close and tipped her face up to his. He could smell the warm, sweet scent of her body, see the little gold specks in those amber eyes. "I just need you to accept that right now, I can't say yes to you. Right now, I still don't know if we could make it together in the long run."

He took her by the shoulders—with care, but with firmness, too. "How 'bout this? *You* don't know— but *I* do. We can make it. Take my word for it."

She groaned a little, and not with passion. "Oh, Tate. Just because you say it doesn't make it so. And besides, *I* have to be sure, too. And I'm not. Not yet."

He wondered, as he'd wondered a thousand times before, how a woman so smooth and soft to the touch, a woman who smelled so sweet and looked so good, could be so damn difficult ninety-nine percent of the time. He whispered low, "Take a chance. Make the leap."

"I wish that I could." She spoke equally softly, searching his face. "I truly do."

He gripped her shoulders harder as he had that all-too-familiar urge to shake her. She winced. He knew he was holding on too tight—and the ring he still had in his hand was poking her. He released her, letting his arms drop to his sides. "You wish that you could," he muttered. "A *wish* and five bucks will get you a lottery ticket—and a one-in-ten-million chance you could win."

She chewed on that plump bottom lip of hers. "Tate, I just can't. Not yet..."

Yelling at her never got him anywhere, he reminded himself for the umpteenth time. He had to take what she'd given him, paltry as it was, and do what he could with it. "But you do think you could. In time."

She raised her hand and laid it, so lightly, on the side of his face. "Oh, I hope so."

She *hoped*. She *wished*.

He caught her wrist, hard—then forced himself to loosen his grip. Gently but firmly, he pushed her cradling hand away from his face. Then he bent to pick up the velvet ring case. He set the ring in its slot and snapped the case shut. It made a sharp, all-too-final kind of sound. He rose to his height and laid the case on the bureau.

"So then, Molly. What about right now?" He turned to her again. "What about tonight?"

"Oh, Tate…" Her eyes had a look in them—kind of velvety and melting. A look that said *yes*.

At least for tonight…

Heat sizzled through him.

Tonight. He wanted that. A lot.

Too bad it wasn't enough.

All you're getting, buddy, he thought. *It'll have to be enough for now.*

And hey, with just a little bit of sugarcoating, he could tell himself he was doing okay, making real progress.

She'd come home with him openly, hadn't she? She was here in his bedroom, wasn't she?

And she did have that soft, hungry look in her eyes, that look that said she didn't want to leave.

He reached for her, hooking his arm low at her waist, reeling her in.

She didn't object as he hauled her up tight against him. He felt the soft fullness of her breasts pressing into his chest. Heat arrowed through him. She gasped—a tiny, needful sound.

He tipped up her stubborn chin. "Kiss me, Molly."

"I—"

"Just shut up and kiss me."

Chapter Eleven

With an ardent cry, Molly lifted her sweet, plump mouth.

Tate took it. Hard. He speared his tongue against the tender seam where her lips met. She opened instantly. He swept the secret inner surfaces, claiming in fact what she wouldn't give him by law, bending her body back, leaning over her, holding her so tight he squeezed the breath from her chest, grinding himself into her...

His hard kiss proved nothing, and he knew it.

He was bigger and stronger and richer. And male. He was supposed to be the one with the power.

Yet somehow, Molly O'Dare foiled him royally at every turn.

He went on kissing her, guiding her backward over his cradling arm. She didn't struggle, didn't squirm, didn't put up the tiniest squeak of protest.

Not Molly. Oh, no.

When Molly gave her body, she gave it all the way. She grabbed for the ruffles on his half-open shirt and she dragged him down with her.

He fell the last few feet, ending up bracing them both on one hand. Slowly his mouth locked hard with hers, he lowered them the rest of the way. They stretched out on the old red Kelim rug.

Now that he knew for sure she wasn't going anywhere, he dared to lift his mouth from hers enough to offer, "Here—or the bed?"

She laughed. The sound echoed through him, making every nerve vibrate with hunger and heat. He pressed his hips harder against her. He was fully erect and aching to bury himself deep inside her.

She pushed at his shoulders, guiding him over, wanting the top position—which was no surprise. He let her have it, rolling to his back so she could climb on and straddle him. She took the sides of his shirt— and ripped it wide.

Buttons went flying. One just missed hitting him in the eye.

"Watch it," he warned.

She was yanking at his sleeves, first one and then the other. "Here first," she whispered, a half smile curling her kiss-swollen lips. She got the shirt off him and shoved it away, then splayed her hands flat on his chest and caressed him, rubbing back and forth on him with her hips as she ran her hands over his exposed chest. His heart was exploding—and so was what she was sitting on. "Bed later…" She groaned, grabbing his arms, pressing them wide and down to the rug and then lowering her head to lick at his chest. She bit his left nipple.

And he groaned, too. "I was…getting kind of fond of that shirt."

She sat up tall on him then. He let out a low cry at the sweet agony of her feminine heat, pressing down all around him. "Shh," she said, "shh," her fingers on his mouth. He sucked those fingers inside. "I'll…buy you another one," she promised, as he teased her fingers with the tip of his tongue. She was still rocking her hips on him, hard and sweet and slow.

He knew he had to get her naked pretty quick—or he would lose it just from the burning friction all that rubbing created. He grabbed for her tight little shirt and hauled it upward. She got the message, taking the sides of it from him, yanking it over her head and throwing it halfway across the room.

She slid back a little, onto his thighs, and she pulled her wet fingers from his mouth and got busy with his fly. She yanked it open and then rose to her knees so he could lift his hips, ease his boxers over his rock-hard erection and get his pants down.

They hung up on his boots. Swearwords echoed in his shattered mind. It was ridiculous, this business of getting out of their clothes. It took too long. Much, much too long.

Molly was already handling the problem. She scooted off him and took one boot and then the other, bracing herself and falling backward as each boot came free of his foot. After the boots, she whipped his socks off, twirling each one like a lasso and sending it sailing with a husky, "Yahoo!"

They laughed together—it was slightly frantic and very hungry, their laughter. She got rid of his pants and boxers and then fell forward, onto all fours, arms braced on either side of his knees. She gave him the once-over, her gaze moving up his naked body. When she met his eyes, she winked.

"Get back here," he commanded.

She didn't put up even token resistance, only slid up his body and planted herself smack on top of the crucial equipment.

Neither of them was laughing by then.

He reached behind her, got a hold of the twin hooks at the back of her bra. A quick flick and those hooks fell open. He got the bra by the front and pulled. She curved her shoulders in and straightened her arms forward. He pulled the thing off and tossed it away.

"Yeah. Oh, yeah…" He reached up. She leaned in, giving him the weight of those beautiful coral-tipped breasts to hold in his eager hands. Were they fuller than he remembered—fuller and riper, somehow?

He thought so. Pride welled in him. His baby was doing that, changing her, rounding and softening her body even more than before. He rolled her nipples between his fingers as she tossed her head back and rocked harder on top of him.

It was urgent that he get inside her.

But suddenly, it was absolutely vital that he explore her body first, that he see and feel for himself any changes his baby might have been making since the last time he'd laid claim to her. Molding her rib cage, he brought his hands downward, first pressing them open just beneath her breasts. He loved her breasts.

And they looked so white and full and soft in contrast to his man-sized tanned hands.

Molly moaned. She wrapped her fingers around his wrists and she went on rocking, driving him wild. He caressed his way downward. She shut her eyes and tossed her head back, releasing her grip on him, laying her hands on her spread thighs, rocking away. Below her rib cage, the hollow that dipped to her navel wasn't quite as pronounced.

She was filling out. No doubt about it. He unbuttoned her shorts and pulled the zipper wide. She wore her usual satin bikini panties—purple ones this time. Above the satin, her belly was soft and gently rounded.

He placed his hand there, on the silky skin of her stomach. Amazing. His child was inside there.

He'd taken biology in high school. He knew that right now the baby was smaller than the palm of his hand. But would he have passed that stage where he looked like some strange little frog—with webbed hands and a tail?

Tate wasn't sure. Still, he couldn't help picturing a perfect, fat little baby, like the ones you saw in TV commercials. A perfect, fat little baby, curled in a ball and sucking his thumb...

Molly stilled in her rocking. She dipped her head forward, opened lazy eyes—and smiled at him.

"Fuller," he whispered, pressing more firmly against her stomach.

She braced her hands on his shoulders, her wild hair falling forward to tickle his nose. She kissed him, a quick kiss. "Soon I'll be fat as an old heifer, you just watch."

"You'll be beautiful. Always," he said. He moved his hand on her belly—to one side and then back. "When will I be able to feel him kick?"

She kissed him again. "It'll be a few months yet—and didn't I tell you? *She's* a girl."

He'd always figured his first kid would be a son. "We'll see…"

"You don't want a girl?" She was trying to be cool about it. But he could see in her eyes that his answer *would* matter.

He gave her a slow smile. "I suppose I'd end up getting used to a daughter as good lookin' as you."

She kissed his nose. "That was absolutely the perfect thing to say."

"And, hey, it's just possible she'll get my grandmother's disposition."

She faked a glare. "Oh, you…" And she fell on him, tickling.

He squirmed and laughed and pretended, for a minute or two, to be at her mercy. But then he managed, even with all her slithering around, to work his fingers under the elastic of her panties.

She let out a sharp little sound of excited surprise and the tickling stopped. With her crotch pressed to his, her legs folded along his thighs and her head tucked into the crook of his shoulder, she lay still, breathing in sharp, ragged gasps. He nuzzled her hair, so soft and warm, smelling of fragrant shampoo and also faintly of chlorine from the dunking tank.

Oh, yeah. This was good.

This was just right…

He slipped his hand farther down into her panties. She gasped in his ear as he petted the silky curls that

covered her mound. And when he dipped his middle
finger into the satin wetness between her spread
thighs, she groaned.

He urged her hips upward. She lifted a little, giving
him easier access so that he managed to slip the rest
of his fingers down into that hot, wet groove. He
parted the folds, at the same time rubbing at the nub
of her sex with his thumb.

Molly panted harder. She was moving again, rocking against his hand. He slipped a finger all the way
in—and then another after it. She rocked faster,
moaning into his ear. He turned his head enough to
nibble on the skin of her temple.

"Oh, Tate," she whispered between ragged
breaths. "Oh, Tate. Oh, yes..."

He realized he could last a little longer, after all—
now she'd lifted her hips off him and she was doing
her rocking against his hand. He could last long
enough to bring her over the brink at least one time
ahead of him. He liked that, liked pleasuring her.
Liked the feel of her silky wetness, the scent of sex
and woman that radiated off her. He liked her moans
of need, growing ever more urgent, and the ragged,
hungry sound of her breathing.

Most of all he liked that right now there was no
question where she belonged. She was wild and willing now—all his—rocking in his arms.

He pleasured her and he whispered encourage-
ments, naughty words of what it felt like for him to
be touching her like this; rough words of his own
need and how he planned to satisfy it; silky words of
promise that he would never stop...

She rocked harder, all the more frantically—and

then she froze on a strangled little gasp. He felt her tender inner surfaces contract around his fingers and the sudden spill of silky wetness. She reached down between them and grabbed his wrist. He kept his hand still, fingers unmoving within her, letting her have it her way at the last, until the tiny contractions faded down and she went limp on top of him.

"Um," she said, rubbing her breasts against his chest, stretching like a satisfied cat. "Oh, my…"

"Don't get too comfortable," he commanded huskily. "I'm not through with you yet…."

She tipped her head back and licked the side of his jaw. "Your wish—" she swiped her tongue against his ear "—is my command."

"Hold that thought." He wrapped his arms around her, surging up, cradling her to him as he rolled them both over.

He was on top again.

She looked up at him, lips red, cheeks flushed, hair all wild, crackling with static, electric-gold against the deep-red rug. "Oh, Tate," she whispered. And at that moment, his only desire was that she might always say his name that way.

As though she wanted only him, as though she couldn't get enough of him, as though he could have all of her.

Any time, any place, any way that he wanted.

He rose to his knees between her spread thighs and laid both hands at her waist. Slowly, he moved his hands downward, hooking his fingers under the waist of her shorts, catching the panties beneath, as well.

She lifted her legs straight up. He whipped them off. And at last, she was every bit as naked as he was.

He sat back on his haunches and admired the glorious, all-woman shape of her, found pleasure in the gleam of desire in her eyes, in the willing, soft smile on her oh-so-kissable mouth. It came to him powerfully that she satisfied him—and not only when it came to the two of them naked doing what they were doing now.

No. It was something else. Some other, deeper, more mysterious kind of satisfaction. When he had her like this, naked and soft and watching him with that melting *take me* look in her eyes, well, he could do anything. Pass any test. Win any challenge.

All things were possible and all was right with the world.

"Tate?" she said, looking at him sideways, catching her lower lip between her white teeth. "You okay?"

He looked at her some more. He could never get enough of just looking at her.

A little crease had formed between her smooth brows. "Tate?"

"Molly," he whispered low. "Why can't it always be this way?"

She had no answer—only a tiny smile and a low cry and slim, eager arms, reaching up for him.

He went down to her, let her wrap him in her silky embrace. She lifted her long legs and wrapped them around him, too. Her hand slid between their bodies, finding him, guiding him home.

He let out a guttural cry as he entered her. There was nothing—*nothing,* like the feel of her. So tight and wet and slick and hot, all around him now.

He had to hold completely still for a second or two.

He knew if he moved, he would lose it. And he didn't want that.

Not yet, anyway…

When he felt he could bear it, he pulled back slowly—and then bucked into her, hard. She took him eagerly, with a glad cry.

After that, there was only the hot, pulsing river of his own need, driving him harder, sucking him down….

Chapter Twelve

"It would be a kind of...trial run," Molly explained with a sweet, hopeful smile.

They were sharing their first breakfast together—in bed.

Tate sipped his strong black coffee and suggested dryly, "This isn't Hollywood, Molly."

That sweet smile went slightly sour. "Well, Tate. I know that—not that Hollywood has a thing to do with this conversation."

He clarified, "I'm only saying, a trial run at marriage sounds like something they might do in California. Or New York City. But not here in Texas. Here in Texas, you're married or you're not. When it comes to the state of matrimony, *this* state has no trial runs."

"What a *clever* way to put it." She picked up a

triangle of toast and her butter knife. "And isn't it wonderful that we've got no strange or nonsensical laws here in Texas?"

"You bet it is," he blustered, sensing a trap, barreling into it anyway.

She hit him with the punch line. "What about common-law marriages, then?"

He gave her a lowering look. "What the hell about them?"

"Haven't you heard? Right here in Texas, if you live together and call yourselves husband and wife and neither of you happens to already be married to someone else, you are considered to be legally wed. That's as weird as anything that could happen in Hollywood, if you ask me."

Okay, so he never should have made that crack about Hollywood. "Molly, why are we talking about this?"

"Because *you* said—"

"Look here." He set down his coffee and put up both hands, palm out. "I surrender. I'm sure every state has a strange law or two."

"So big of you to admit it—and I have to say, it does send a hot little thrill all through me, hearing you say you surrender…"

"I'll bet." He had a thought. Against his own better judgment, he voiced it. "Is that what you want, then?"

"Surrender?" She wiggled her eyebrows.

"Nice try. I meant a common-law marriage."

She stopped wiggling her eyebrows and frowned. "Why would I want that? Didn't I just explain to you that I'm not *ready* for marriage right yet?"

Valiantly he tried to get her to be more specific. "When, exactly, do you think you *will* be ready?"

She studied the toast she'd been carefully buttering. "I'm only saying that for people like us, there ought to be a trial run when it comes to something as serious as getting married."

"People like *us?* What the hell's wrong with us? Never mind. I don't think I want to know. Instead, why don't you try answering the question I asked a minute ago? You know, the one you skipped right on by, the one where I asked you *when* we could get on with it and get married?"

She gave him a pained look. "Okay, okay…"

"Still waiting…"

She made a couple of delicate snorting sounds and then finally admitted, "I just can't say for certain *when* I'll be ready."

There were a lot of things he could have said right then, most of them consisting of strings of four-letter words. He held those things back. While he was restraining himself, Molly set her knife on the edge of her bread plate and took a big, crunchy bite of toast.

Tate watched her chew, thinking that she was the kind of woman who even looked good when she was eating. A man needed that in his wife, to be able to look at her doing something that wasn't ordinarily all that attractive and still want to keep *on* looking.

He glanced toward the window, where the morning sun slanted in through the open curtains.

Aside from the current topic of conversation, it was a damn good moment. Sharing breakfast in bed with Molly. It was almost as good as waking up an hour ago and finding her asleep beside him. During their secret affair, she was always up and gone well before daylight.

She looked so sweet in the morning—all rumpled and soft and pretty. And she had beard burn on her jaw.

He couldn't resist leaning over and kissing the tender spot. "Does it hurt?"

She gave him a devilish smile. "It's nothing. Last night, though. Now, *that* was *something...*"

"That's what I like to hear."

She kissed his lips—a quick, sweet peck. Then she picked up her cup and sipped the herbal tea Miranda had brewed for her. "Back to us living together..."

"I've got it." He hit his forehead with the heel of his hand. "Why don't we just get married instead?"

She bit off more toast, chewed it and swallowed. "Were you born with a thick head—or did it get that way gradually?"

"I don't see the sense in this, that's all. What good's it gonna do for us to try out being married?"

"Well, we'll learn more about each other, for one thing. We'll see if we can stand to be together, day in and day out. And we'll do it without being locked into anything too permanent."

"What's wrong with permanent? You're having my baby. You need something permanent."

"Tate, we're not going to get anywhere if you start telling me what I need."

He slumped back against the pillows and glared at his breakfast. "I just don't like it."

She let the sheet slip lower to reveal her beautiful bare breasts, and she looked at him with her eyelids droopy and her mouth all soft, lips slightly parted...

He felt the covers start to tent beneath his tray.

No, he thought. *Down, boy.* He folded his arms over his chest. "I suppose you think you can get me to do anything—just by flashing me a little skin and giving me that come-and-get-it look."

She canted over close and whispered in his ear. "We *will* be together. Right here. In your house. Every night. And weekends—and in the mornings, like now. We'll do our very best to make it work between us. And then, well, in a couple of months, if we find out that we're—"

"Hold it."

Droopy-eyed and sleep-rumpled, the covers down around her waist, she waited for him to continue. Damn, but she knew how to work him when she put her mind to it....

He ordered his libido to keep the hell out of this—where was he? Oh, yeah...

"A couple of *months?* You'll be practically ready to have the baby by then."

"Five months along is hardly ready to have the baby—and anyway, maybe it'll be sooner. Maybe we'll find that it's all working out and—"

"How?"

"Er...what?"

"How will we know that it's working out? What's going to make you decide you're finally willing to take the big plunge and marry me?"

She pulled the sheet back up so he couldn't see her pretty, puckered nipples anymore. "Well, Tate, I don't know yet. I'll just...know that I know, when I know..."

Tate grabbed his coffee and took another sip—a

big one, and wished he'd told Miranda to pour a little whiskey in it. He plunked the cup back on the tray. "Has it ever occurred to you, Molly, that you've got something real strange going on in your head when it comes to the prospect of saying those two little words, 'I' and 'do'?"

She fiddled with her toast, picked up her tea again and then set it down without drinking from it. "You know, you're right. Having never really known what marriage is, I find it pretty terrifying to think of letting myself get locked into one. I've got this scary kind of certainty inside myself that I'm going to be really bad at it."

He could hardly believe it. She'd just *admitted* he was right about something. *Remember this moment,* he thought reverently. *With Molly, moments like this won't be coming around all that often.*

And even if she'd agreed with him on this one tiny point, her agreement didn't bring her any closer to accepting his ring on her finger, now did it? In fact, it only pushed the possibility further away.

"Please, Tate…" She leaned in close again. Her breath smelled of peppermint tea. Her skin had a velvety, rose-petal kind of glow. "Can we try this? Please? I do want to make it work with you, in a forever sort of way. I just…I need to kind of slip into it slow."

He looked at her tempting mouth—and then up into her hopeful, shining eyes.

He was weakening and he knew it. He was thinking that if he went along with her on this, at least she would *be* here. In his bed. In his house…

No, it wasn't all he wanted from her. It wasn't all their baby *needed* from her.

But it was better than a poke in the eye with a sharp stick, now wasn't it?

He reached for her, hooking his hand around her neck, spearing his fingers up into her tangled hair and bringing her adorable face right up to his. "Say I agreed to this…"

Her eyes went all dewy. "Oh, Tate…"

He tightened his fingers in her hair. "Just *say* I did. You'd move in today?"

"Yes. I would. This very afternoon. I have to work from eleven to four. But after that, I'll go right home and pack up some things and… Oh, no." She pushed away from him, frowning.

"What's the matter now?"

"I forgot all about Granny."

Dusty. Now, there was an angle he hadn't tried yet. "Yeah." He put on his most somber expression. "She might not like it, you and me living in sin…"

This time the snorting sound Molly made wasn't delicate in the least. "Oh, knock it off. *Living in sin?* I don't believe you said that."

It *was* kind of overboard, he admitted to himself. *Living in sin.* Like something his grandfather would say during one of his tirades—and damn. If Ol' Tuck was still above ground, there would be one level-five tornado of a tirade about now.

Oh, yeah. Ol' Tuck would've raised holy hell about this entire situation. He would have been furious when he learned that Tate had gotten Molly pregnant. And then thoroughly scandalized at the idea that the Tate heir would even consider proposing marriage to a lowly O'Dare. And that Molly should come to live at the ranch house—and sleep in Tate's bed—*without* benefit of matrimony...

It would have been one Texas-sized battle between Tate and his grandfather over that one, no doubt about it.

And even without his grandfather around to stir the pot, there were still going to be lots of local citizens with their two cents to add.

"Molly, folks *are* gonna talk."

"Let 'em. I'm an O'Dare, remember? Most of the gossips in town think my family's main purpose in life is to give them something to yammer on about. I learned a long time ago not to let them get to me— and never, under any circumstances, to allow what they say to change my way of doing things. And as for my granny, well, we respect each other, or we wouldn't be living in the same house together. She doesn't try to run my life and I don't try to run hers— but I *am* worried that she'll be lonely, on her own at the house."

He hauled her over close again and kissed the tip of her nose. "If that's all you're worried about, there's plenty of room here."

She pulled away and gaped at him, clutching the sheet to her breasts. "You mean it?"

"Hell, yes. She can have a whole damn wing to herself if she wants one. We've got two to spare."

"Tate Bravo, you do have your moments."

"That's a compliment, right?"

"Yes. It is." She added softly, "Thank you."

He hooked his finger under the sheet, down into the little hollow between her ripe breasts, and gave a tug. She let the sheet drop. "Come here," he said, and crooked that finger. "You can show me how grateful you are."

"I have to be at work in—"

"You can show me fast." He reached for her.

She giggled and let him drag her close. Her tray rattled as she hit it with her knee. "Oh, no. What about these trays?"

He laughed and nuzzled her hair. "Not a problem. You can show me *very* carefully…"

"Well, sugar love," Granny said that afternoon when Molly told her she was moving in with Tate. "You'll do what you think is right. I know that."

Molly couldn't help asking, "Do you think I should marry him?"

But Granny didn't fall into that trap. "Like it matters a lick what I think. Uh-uh. This is your decision." They were sitting on the sofa, side by side. Granny reached over and patted Molly's knee. "You'll be fine, don't you worry. Just keep true to what you know is right."

"Well, I don't want to rush into this, that's all. I'm nervous about marriage. I really am."

"Honey baby, that's okay. Maybe, in a while, you'll get to like the idea."

"I'll be working on that."

"Well, good. Keep your mind open all the time— and your mouth shut at least fifty percent of the time. You'll do just fine."

Molly took her granny's skinny, age-spotted hand. "We'd like it very much if you came and stayed with us. It was Tate's suggestion. He says you can have a whole wing to yourself if you want it.''

Granny leaned close to Molly and kissed Molly's forehead—and then gently pulled her hand free. ''Well, that's real sweet. But you know what? I wouldn't mind at all having this fine house of yours to myself for a while—that is, if *you* don't mind my stayin' here.''

Molly started to argue that Granny would be happier with her and Tate—but then she noticed the twinkle in Granny's eyes. ''Granny. What have you and Skinny Jordan been up to?''

Was that a blush on Granny's lined cheeks? Sure did look like it. ''Skinny Jordan is a fine man. Agreeable and down-to-earth and loyal as they come…''

''A little like Andy Devine?'' Molly suggested softly.

''That's right,'' said Granny. ''A whole dang lot like Andy Devine.''

Tate and Molly had dinner in the formal dining room that night, just the two of them at the long, heavily-carved beechwood table with its sixteen leather-seated nail-head-trimmed chairs. Tate had instructed Miranda to put out the best china and his grandmother's treasured sterling.

Molly laughed when she saw that Miranda had set the two places at either end of the table. ''*Hellllloooo* down there!'' And then she picked up her plate and water glass and carried them down to his end, returning to her end to get the silver and her napkin. ''There now.'' She shook out the napkin and smoothed it on her lap. "Isn't that better?" Tate had to admit that it was.

They ate a leisurely meal and then retired to the master suite to make slow, lazy love.

When he woke Sunday morning, there she was. Right beside him.

He could get used to this, he decided. Oh, yeah. He certainly could.

Molly wanted to go to church. So they went and listened to Pastor Partridge drone on for over an hour about the rewards of forgiveness and the milk of loving-kindness. Long sermons always made Tate feel kind of drowsy. But every time he started to drop off, Molly would give him a gentle nudge in the ribs and he would snap to again.

All in all, it wasn't that bad. Yeah, folks stared—and then put on big, wide smiles and nodded all friendlylike when Tate caught them doing it. But he didn't let the stares get to him. He just smiled and nodded in return. Once he and Molly were married, all the gossip would die down and folks would find something else to stare at.

That night, Molly had one of her committee meetings. Tate worked in his study until about nine-thirty, checking on the income from the leases. Most of the quarter-million acres that had once been the Double T Ranch were now leased out to other ranchers, to oil companies and farmers. Tate made a hefty profit off those leases.

About nine-thirty, the phone rang. He picked it up.

"Tate Bravo here."

"You don't say?"

"Tucker?" Tate sat up straighter. "That really you?"

He heard the familiar wry chuckle. "Last time I checked, it was."

"I don't believe it. How long's it been?"

"Too long."

Tate braced his elbows on the desk and frowned. "No problem with the money, is there?"

"None at all. It shows up in that account you set up for me every month, regular as clockwork, and plenty of it, too. I live like a damn mogul—not bad for a man who's never had a job to speak of."

Tate didn't approve of his brother's wandering ways. But he knew what was fair. As the one who stayed home and took care of business, it was Tate's responsibility to see to it that Tucker always got his share. "Half of what Grandfather left behind belongs to you. Any time you need more than you're getting—"

"Stop right there. I've got plenty of money and that's not why I'm calling."

"So what's up?"

"You sitting down?"

Tate felt his frown return. "Sitting down? What's the problem?"

"Relax. It's good news—or at least, *I* think it is…"

Tate had just hung up with Tucker and was still shaking his head in disbelief over what his brother had told him, when Molly arrived home at ten. He heard her let herself in the front door and then a series of beeping sounds as she struggled to reset the alarm.

After that, he heard her heels tapping on the granite floor, moving his way. And then there she was, leaning in the doorway, faking a scowl. "I may have to dig out Granny's shotgun and eliminate that alarm."

He sat back in his chair and drank in the welcome sight of her. "You'll get used to it."

"You'd better hope I do, or one of these days you'll be dealing with a missing alarm box and a big hole in the wall. I just don't see the point in those things, I truly don't."

"We had some idiot break in here a while back. No real harm done but scared the hell out of Miranda. Can't have that. And then there's the fact that if I caught someone at it, they would have a hole in them from the .38 I keep in the bottom drawer of this desk. Uh-uh. Better if the alarm just scares them off."

Molly peeled herself off the door frame and came sauntering toward him, detouring once she reached his desk and crossing around behind him. At his back, she bent down and wrapped her arms around his neck. As always, her scent tempted him, and the feel of her soft arms around him caused a tightness in his chest— not to mention in his trousers.

"Making lots of money?" she asked into his ear.

He let out a low noise in the affirmative, turning his head so he could capture her lips. They shared a long, deep kiss. He held her mouth as he slowly spun in his chair, guiding her back out of the way with his hands at her waist and then pulling her close once he was on his feet.

"Well," she said, looking up at him all lazy-eyed, when they finally broke for air. "That was about the nicest welcome home I ever got."

"I can do better."

And with that, he swept her high in his arms and carried her straight to the bedroom.

Later, they raided the freezer and sat at the kitchen counter eating ice cream from the carton, sharing a spoon. She told him about her committee meeting, and he told her that his brother, Tucker, had called.

"Finally got his law degree," Tate said. "He actually passed the bar—and that's not all."

She scooped up a bite of ice cream and offered it to him. He took it off the spoon. She predicted, "Either he's getting married—or he's decided to move back home."

He swallowed and took the spoon from her. "How did you know that?"

She laughed. "Just guessing—and you didn't say which one it was."

He scooped out another bite and held it out for her. "Well, as far as I know, he's *not* getting married."

She opened her mouth and he slid the spoon inside. "Mmm," she said and swallowed. "I love chocolate. So. Your baby brother is coming home to stay."

"Yeah—or at least, that's what he says right now. He has been prone, over the years, to change his mind. So I won't really believe it until I see it." He stared off toward the central island. "I always thought it kind of…mixed him up, you know? Never knowing who his father really was…" He looked at her again, watching to see if he'd hit a nerve with that one.

But she seemed to take it well. She teased, "Oh, I get it. So since I don't know who *my* daddy was, that would make me mixed up, too?"

"Now, I didn't say that."

"Maybe not. But I think you *meant* that—at least a little." Before he could think of a comeback, she added, "Didn't your mother always claim that your father was Tucker's dad, too?"

He made a low sound. "Come on. Since my father died before *I* was born, that doesn't seem real probable."

"Yep, that is pretty odd."

"Molly, it goes beyond odd and straight through to impossible. The story was that she—"

"Your mother?"

"That's right. My mother. She saw her long-dead husband at an OU-Texas game that Grandfather and Grandmother dragged her to. When she spotted him, she told Ol' Tuck she had to use the rest room—and then she never came back to her seat in the stands. She vanished. For two weeks. And then she showed up here with some wild story of how she'd been off with her husband. Then, nine months after that, Tucker was born."

"Hmm. Romantic. Like a passion that could never die."

"Romantic. Right. About as romantic as a train wreck. My take is, she maybe saw some guy who looked like my father. Maybe she even convinced herself that the man she saw *was* the husband she'd lost five years before. Who knows what went on in my mother's head? Logic was a concept foreign to her nature. I think she ran off with this guy who looked like my father and eventually he dumped her—or she decided she wanted to head back home.

Whatever. She wouldn't let go of the idea that Tucker was my father's son, too.''

"I still think it's romantic.''

"Call it whatever the hell you want. We're never going to know what happened for certain. All the people who might know are gone, now." He felt her big toe, tickling its way up the side of his leg. "Watch it," he warned.

She fluttered her eyelashes. "Oh, I do intend to…and I think you are a little bit smug, Tate Bravo. Just because you're sure your mama married your daddy before you were born, you think that makes you less mixed up than me or your brother."

"Smug? I am not. But I do believe that kids have a right to parents who are married."

She leaned close enough that he could smell the chocolate on her breath. "I have an idea. Let's not go there, okay? Not tonight."

"Humph," he said.

"Tell me more about Tucker. Please? What's made him decide to finally come home?"

He let several seconds of silence elapse before he gave in and answered her question. "He said he's seen enough of the big, wide world. He wants to come home and hang out a shingle over on Center Street."

"Well, well. Start his own law practice in his hometown?"

"Yeah. But then I remembered that Leland Hogan was getting close to retiring." Leland had been the Tate family attorney for as long as Tate could remember. "I figure Tucker could go in with Leland, pick up the slack at first, and then take the reins once Leland's ready to work on his golf game full-time. Good

for both of them. Tucker gets a head start on his practice, and Leland gets a way to keep his clients in the
firm he started when he goes.''

She took the spoon from him, and dipped up a bite
for herself. ''Did your brother go for the idea?''

''He's interested. I'll talk to Leland, then hook up
the two of them. They'll take it from there.''

''When will Tucker be here?''

''Three weeks. He's got to wrap things up in Los
Angeles, he said—that's where he lives now, for the
past year or so.''

Molly fed him another big bite. Then she stuck the
spoon upright in the carton of ice cream and propped
her chin on her fist. ''Who would have thought it?
The famous wandering Tucker Bravo, coming on
home, at last.''

Tate swallowed the icy treat and shook his head.
''I can't believe it, myself.''

''He'll be moving in here, of course...''

He liked the way she said that, with no hesitation
and a happy smile. Molly was a family kind of gal.
Once she married him, he knew she would be looking
out for Tucker just as if Tucker was her own brother.
By the same token, Tate would be taking responsibility for Dusty and Dixie and Ray. But that was okay
with him. Hell. Hadn't he already done what he could
for them?

''Yeah,'' Tate said. ''Tucker'll live here. He wants
the South Wing. He said he likes that big main bedroom in back. Looks out on a little grove of pecan
trees.''

''Sounds nice.'' She nodded toward the open ice-
cream carton. ''Had enough?''

He gave her a long look, from the top of her temptingly mussed hair down over the robe she'd tossed on when they'd gotten out of bed. "I can never get enough…"

She gave him the elbow. "I meant of the ice cream, and you know it, too."

He caught her arm. "C'mere."

She giggled and squirmed—and then she gave in and let him kiss her, which he did with great thoroughness. But when he started pulling on the tie at her waist, she pushed at his chest. "You just wait a minute."

He let her go long enough to put the ice cream in the freezer. Then he grabbed her hand and hauled her back to the bedroom, where he showed her in detail how very glad he was to have her around.

An hour or so later, before they finally dropped off to sleep, she whispered lazily, "So how's the South Wing, anyway? In good condition?"

"Nothing wrong with it that I know of. Had the roof replaced a couple of years ago. And the foundation is solid."

"I meant is it all ready for your long-lost brother to move in?"

He shrugged. "Far as I know. Miranda keeps an eye on it for me. She'd have said if there was something that needed looking after."

"But just to be certain, we should check it out, don't you think, before he comes?"

We. That sounded damn good to him. "Sure. I'll have Miranda take the drapes off the furniture and we can go have look."

"We might want to spiff things up a little—rearrange the furniture, see about fresh paint in a room or two, just so it looks welcoming, you know?''

There was the *we* word again. They were getting closer to working things out, oh yeah, they were. In no time at all, she would be telling him yes, walking down the aisle to meet him, wearing a long white dress and a smile that said she was his for the rest of their lives.

He had the bright idea to go for it—to try once more, right then and there.

He pressed a kiss against her sweet-smelling hair, snuggled her closer in the circle of his arm and whispered, ''Molly?''

She stroked his chest. ''Hmm?''

''We're getting along real good, now, aren't we?''

She brushed a soft kiss in the hollow of his shoulder. ''Um-hmm...''

''So...what about it? Let's stop putting it off. Let's get married. What do you say?''

Nothing. *That* was what she said. And he knew instantly, by the way her hand stopped caressing his chest, by the way her body tightened in his hold, that he'd jumped the gun—again.

At last, she heaved a heavy sigh. ''Oh, Tate, I...'' She didn't finish. Not that she needed to.

''You can cut it right there,'' he growled. ''That *Oh, Tate* about said it all.'' He rolled his head on the pillow, so he was looking away from her.

She caught his chin, guided it back around to her. ''Come on. It's only two days since I moved in.''

He knew he should say something namby-pamby like, *It's okay. I understand,* and leave it at that. But he couldn't make himself let it be. ''And we've been doing fine,'' he insisted. ''Better than fine. I was just thinking that it ought to be pretty damn obvious to you, from how good it's been the last two days, that you don't have to be afraid of the idea of being my wife.''

She only softly repeated, ''Two days. It's not enough. We're still smack-dab in the honeymoon period. Sure, we'll get along for a while. That's pretty much a guarantee. We're both trying hard, on our best behavior. But we won't be able to keep that up forever. It's how we do in the long run that matters.''

He looked hard into her eyes. ''Two questions. How can you have a honeymoon when you're not married yet—and how damn long is the long run?''

All she said to that was, ''Oh, Tate.''

He swore low. ''Damn you, Molly. I've heard about enough *Oh, Tates* for one night. And you haven't answered either of my questions, now have you?''

She didn't answer that question, either. She just pried his hand from around her shoulders and sat up.

''Get back down here,'' he commanded—and realized his error when she instantly swung her feet to the rug and rose from the bed. He blustered on. ''Molly, I mean it. Get back here.''

She sent him a look over her glorious bare shoulder. That look said what he probably should have known by then: ordering her around wouldn't get him anything but further away from his goal of getting a ring on her finger.

She started walking—around the end of the bed and toward the bathroom. He watched her go, thinking how furious she made him, how good she looked naked—and how he would be better off at this point to just keep his damn mouth shut.

At *this* point? Hell. He'd have been better off if he'd kept his mouth shut, period.

The door to the master bath and dressing room clicked carefully closed behind her. Tate stared at the shadow of that door for a while, feeling all cold and bleak inside, wondering if she would ever take the big leap and say yes to him.

Times like this, he had serious doubts. He was a man used to taking what he wanted, and she was a woman who didn't give an inch. What real chance was there that the two of them would ever find a common ground?

Right then, alone in his bed, with the woman he wanted on the other side of the bathroom door, he had a minute or two where he couldn't help feeling that they would never work things out.

But Tate Bravo was of tough pioneering stock—born, bred and raised to look to the future with an eye toward success. He'd never been a man to let his attitude stay negative for long.

He had her where he wanted her now, didn't he? She lived in his house and she slept in his bed. When she finally came out of the bathroom, he would treat her real gentle and force himself to grate out an apology for ordering her around.

She would forgive him. She could be a fireball—but she *was* trying, in her own frustrating way, to give the two of them a chance.

Right about then, the bathroom door opened. Slowly. The wedge of golden light from inside grew larger as the door opened wider.

Finally Molly peeked around it, her hair a halo of spun silk framing her shadowed face. With the light behind her, he couldn't see her expression and he had a moment of stark fear that she would tell him it was over, that she couldn't deal with him constantly pressuring her and ordering her around. She was going back to her little house on Bluebonnet Lane and they could talk about his visitation rights as soon as the baby was born.

But then she said in a teasing tone, "Is it safe to come out now?" and all at once, he could breathe again—when he hadn't even realized that for a moment there, his lungs had stopped working.

He sucked in a big, healthy breath of air and when he let it out, he said, in a growl, "Look. I'm sorry. I've got no right to go giving you orders."

She shot out that door so fast, he couldn't help but smile. She darted to her side of the bed and jumped up beside him, yanking up the covers and slithering inside. Cuddling up good and close, she kissed him on the edge of his jaw. "I accept your apology."

And then she kissed him square on the mouth.

Tate wrapped his arms around her and kissed her back, tucking her into him, pressing himself against her softness, feeling his sex start to rise. She really got to him, Molly did. One sweet kiss from her and he was ready to go—again. He sucked on her neck and she groaned in pleasure.

He began kissing his way downward, stopping to lavish attention on her full, white breasts. And then heading lower still, licking his way down the middle of her, over her rounded stomach where his baby lay sleeping, to the nest of gleaming gold curls, so silky and inviting, at the juncture of her thighs...

A few minutes later, as he rolled her beneath him and buried himself in her softness, in that split second before all conscious awareness flew right out the window, he thought that they really were working things out between them.

In no time at all, she would be telling him yes.

Chapter Thirteen

But Molly didn't say yes.

She remained in his house and she spent her nights in his arms. She was passionate and attentive to him and, as long as Tate didn't try to boss her, she was easy to get along with. But every time he dared to bring up the subject of marriage, he got a lot of regretful words and at the end of them, a *no*.

Tate didn't get it.

They worked so well together. As a team, they approached the task of making the South Wing more inviting for Tucker when he got home.

Miranda took the covers off the furniture over there and gave it a thorough cleaning. Then Tate and Molly spent a couple of evenings moving stuff around. Tate's grandmother had done most of the decorating. She had an eye for the ornate. There was way too much gold leaf—not to mention an excess of crystal chandeliers. They chose a bunch of pieces to put into storage and raided the other wings of the house for some simpler-looking stuff. Molly decided that the forty-year-old flocked velvet wallpaper had to go. She hired a crew to steam it off and then chose fresh colors and got the painters in. The wing was ready for Tucker a week before he was scheduled to arrive.

And they had some fine times.

On a hot Friday evening, they drove out to a steakhouse Tate knew of in Abilene and took Dusty and Skinny along. The food was good and the conversation lively.

Dusty couldn't wait to get Molly in the air with her. "Soon as I get my license, I'm taking you up, sugar hon."

Molly cut a bite of steak and gave Dusty a worried look. "I don't think so. Not for a while, anyway."

"Well, sweetie pie, how long's a while?"

"Oh, say maybe in twenty years or so. I want to be sure my baby girl gets raised up right before I go flying with *you*, Granny."

Dusty leaned Skinny's way. "She says that now, but you wait. I'll talk her into it, you just watch."

Skinny nodded. "I know you will, darlin'." The look on his face said that Dusty could do anything— and he was one lucky man to be allowed to stand at her side while she did it.

Dixie and Ray had them over to dinner at the double-wide. Dixie wasn't much of a cook. They had macaroni and cheese from a box and a salad out of a bag. But the quality of the cuisine didn't matter, Tate decided. It was the company that counted, and Tate really was beginning to think of Molly's crazy family as his.

Ray smiled in quiet pride at the way things were working out at the hardware store. Why, he'd even finally got the hang of how to make change. And just the day before, Ray reported, Davey Luster had trusted him to track down a lost order of three-penny nails.

"Now I'm a married man," said Ray, "I finally got me a reason to stay focused on the job. My reason is Dixie—and our future as husband and wife." He patted Dixie's hand and they shared a moony-eyed glance. "I got you to thank, Tate, for setting me up. And Dixie and me will always be grateful."

"Yes, we will," said Dixie, granting Tate her gorgeous smile and a look of deepest appreciation.

Molly beamed at him, looking kind of dewy-eyed herself. Even Dixie's one-eyed cat seemed to regard him admiringly. Tate felt like the king of the world.

He picked up his juice glass of jug wine and saluted Ray. "Glad to be of help," he said modestly.

A few nights later, Tate took Molly to the Throckleford Country Club's annual Cattlemen's Ball. He had to admit, it wasn't as enjoyable as the evening at Dixie's or the night out with Dusty and Skinny. Some of the wives treated Molly kind of cold. But she sailed on through it and later that night, when they were home and settled in under the covers, she joked that some of those women had ice water in their veins.

"I kind of feel sorry for their poor husbands. How'd you like to climb into bed and find a block of ice waiting there every night of your life?"

Tate chuckled and allowed that he wouldn't like that one bit. He pulled her in close to him. She was all warmth and all woman. He pondered how he ever could have imagined wanting a wife like his grandmother; a woman with the right name and the right connections, one who would be queen of the country club wives.

Funny how little it mattered now that he would never have that kind of bride. Now, he only wanted one woman.

If only she would quit stalling and marry him. Time was flying by. Why now, even wearing all her clothes, if you looked twice, you could see that Molly's stomach was getting rounder....

That night, in bed after the ball, he seriously considered bringing up the subject of marriage—again. But he was getting pretty tired of being told no.

And Molly was lifting up her mouth to him, eager for his kiss. He pressed his lips to hers and put all his attention into making love to her. It worked. For a while, at least, he was able to push the ever-present question of when—and if—she would finally say yes from his mind.

On the Monday after the Cattlemen's Ball, while a freak summer thunderstorm raged outside, Molly and Tate took their places at the table in the dining room, and Miranda began serving the meal. The doorbell chimed as lightning flared through the room. After the big clap of thunder that followed, Tate tucked his napkin under the rim of his plate. "I'll get it, Miranda."

When he opened the front door, his long-lost

brother blew in on a crack of thunder and a hard gust
of wind.

"Whew. Never thought I'd make it." Tucker let
out a laugh. "It's wild out there." He set down his
suitcases and ran his hand back through his short,
spiky-looking brown-gold hair.

Tate shut the door, muffling the loud booms of
thunder and the hollow drumming of the heavy rain.
"We wondered where the hell you were."

"We got out of LAX late, then circled the Dallas
airport for a couple of hours, waiting on a break in
the weather. I would have called, but my cell was as
dead as yesterday's news. I keep telling myself I've
got to remember to charge the damn thing."

Tucker looked good, Tate thought. He'd filled out
some since the last time he'd been home, for their
mother's funeral two years before. A little thicker
through the shoulders and bigger in the arms—which
were extended toward Tate.

"Well, big brother, do I get a welcome-home
hug?"

Tate stepped forward and he and Tucker did a little
mutual back thumping. When that was over, Tucker
spotted Molly, who'd come to stand in the arch to the
dining room by then.

"Hey." Tucker blinked, clearly puzzled. "Well,
what do you know? Molly, right? Molly O'Dare.
Didn't we go to high school together?"

Molly came toward them wearing her widest,
friendliest smile. "You were in the class right after
mine, I think. Hello, Tucker. Welcome home."

Yeah, okay. Tate knew he probably should have
explained to his brother about how Molly was living

with him. But he and Tucker had only talked a couple of times since Tucker decided to come back home. The right opportunity to go into the situation had never presented itself.

Tucker released Molly's hand and slanted Tate a look. "So...how's life treating you?"

"Great," Tate blustered, "just great." He took Molly by the arm and pulled her to his side, feeling as though he should say something right then about their relationship—but not knowing what.

Maybe...

Molly here's having my baby and she's going to marry me—eventually. I think...

Or...

Molly and I are living together. It's a trial run for marriage...

Uh-uh. Any way he put it, it was going to sound peculiar. Better to just save all the explaining for later.

Molly wrapped an arm around his waist and laid her other hand on his chest, in a move both casual and intimate. She seemed so...happy and comfortable about it all. She said to Tucker, "We're just sitting down to eat. Why don't you leave your suitcases right here, and Jesse will carry them over to the South Wing for you? You can use the half bath off the breakfast room if you want to freshen up a little."

"Great idea. I could eat a whole herd of Herefords, Hmm...something smells like beef."

"Prime rib," Molly told him.

"Be with you in a flash." Tucker was already headed for the half bath in back.

Once his brother was out of sight, Tate tried to turn for the dining room. Molly didn't let him go. She gave a squeeze to his waist and she tugged on the collar of his shirt.

"You should have told him about me, don't you think?" She said it low, just between the two of them. And she didn't look the least upset. More like kind of sweetly amused.

That bugged him. Yeah, all right. He should have said something to Tucker. But he'd kept hoping that before Tucker arrived Molly would finally say yes, that he would be able to introduce her as his bride.

No such luck. And now she found it *amusing* that she refused him at every turn?

She must have known by his expression that *he* was not the least amused. "Whatever you're thinking," she whispered in warning, "save it for later, please."

He declined to reply to that. "What do you say we head on back to the table?"

"You bet." Her arm dropped away from his waist and she let go of his collar.

They turned—side by side, but not touching—and went in to dinner.

The meal went well enough. They ate to the accompaniment of gusting rain spattering the windows and bright lightning flashes, followed by booming rolls of thunder. Tate tried to put his newly stirred-up resentment toward Molly aside.

Molly herself was charming and talkative. Tucker praised the food and told them about his life in Los Angeles—and before that in New York and Chicago, in London and Paris and Rome.

After the dessert of apple crisp and homemade ice

cream, Molly excused herself. She had a "few things" that needed "taking care of," she said.

Tate knew it was just an excuse to give him and his brother a little time alone. She got up and said good-night to Tucker and then she looked at Tate with a soft little smile.

"I'll see you later..."

"Yeah," he said, still put out with her, though not as much as before.

They had a good thing going, and he knew it. He just wanted to make it better, make it legal—and make it *right*. When would she see that?

He and Tucker retired to his study across the entry hall, leaving the table for Miranda to clear. Tate poured them each a snifter of brandy and they moved to the sitting area, getting comfortable in a pair of leather wing chairs, with their feet propped up on the wide tufted ottoman that doubled as a coffee table.

They talked about Tucker's prospective partnership with Leland Hogan. The three of them—Tucker, Leland and Tate—would be having dinner at Tres Erisos on Wednesday night. The meal would give Leland and Tucker a first chance to take each other's measure, up close and personal.

"I'm excited about this," Tucker said. "I think it could work out, be a good thing for both Leland and me."

Tate agreed.

They got to talking about the South Wing. Tucker joked about their grandmother and her love of the ornate.

And Tate said, "Molly and I have been working on that one. We had most of the brocade-and-gold-leaf stuff hauled out of there. And the flocked wall-paper is gone, too. I'm guessing you'll want to make more changes. But it's a head start, anyway.''

"I appreciate that." Tucker looked into his snifter. "You know, it was something of a surprise, finding Molly O'Dare here…''

Tate grunted. "'Something of a surprise.' By God, Tuck, you've gone and gotten diplomatic. When did that happen?''

Tucker settled deeper into his chair. "I'm as dip-lomatic as the next guy—as long as I get answers to the questions I ask.''

"Well, you didn't used to be. Time was, you rarely opened your mouth without inserting your foot.''

Tucker nodded. "I remember. I was always giving Ol' Tuck another reason to lay his belt to my back-side. And, Tate?''

"Yeah?''

"Are you going to tell me about Molly, or not?''

Tate toasted his brother with his brandy glass. "Now, there you go. That's more like the trouble-making little brother I remember. If it pops into your head, just open your mouth and let it out. Never, un-der any circumstances, hold back. Never give a thought to the fact that the subject in question might be none of your damn business.''

A smile pulled at the corner of Tucker's full-lipped mouth. "Why am I getting the feeling you don't want to talk about Molly?'' Tate let a grumbling sound be the answer to that. "She's living here with you, right?''

"Do you *ever* take a hint?''

"Well. Is she?''

"Yeah," Tate gave out grudgingly, wondering when the hell his brother would finally butt out—and also, on a deeper level, kind of thinking he wouldn't mind discussing the problem with someone he could trust.

Tucker kept after it. "I'm a little confused. This is just not your style."

"What's not?" As soon as he asked the question, Tate wished he hadn't—seeing as how Tucker went right ahead and answered.

"It's not your style to live with a woman you're not married to, and to do it openly, too, right here in Ol' Tuck's house."

"It's not Grandfather's house anymore, it's *my*— er, I mean, it's *our* house."

Tucker chuckled. "Better watch it. You might end up saying what you really think."

Tate felt kind of small, then. The truth was, deep in his heart, he did think of the house as his. "Sorry. You've been gone a long time."

Tucker looked at him levelly. "I know. And I guess you got a right to a feeling of ownership. You're the one who stayed here, stuck with it, took care of things…"

"A feeling ain't reality. Fact is, this place is yours as much as it's mine." Outside, the rain had stopped. But in the distance, Tate heard the rumble of thunder as it rolled on across the flat, open land. In the silence that followed the thunder, he told his brother, "In spite of your tendency to nose around in things that don't concern you, I'm glad you came back. And I'm hoping you mean it when you say you plan to stick around."

"Thanks…" Tucker's voice was soft, with a thoughtful note. He had a faraway look in his eyes.

Tate sipped his brandy, enjoying the mellow feeling it brought, listening to the distant thunder. He figured his brother had more to say—and he would speak up when he got good and ready to.

Eventually Tucker said, "You know, I spent a lot of years wandering the world, looking for something I never could quite name…" Tucker's voice trailed off again.

Tate sat forward. "Well? Did you find it?"

"No, I didn't."

"So you've given it up—whatever it is?"

"No. I'm still looking. And the last few months, I've started to believe that, whatever it is I'm looking for, it's a lot closer to home than I ever imagined. I'm beginning to understand that what's always been missing from my life isn't out there in some fabulous ancient city halfway 'round the world. I'm thinking— the *more* I think about it—that it's right here, in the town where I grew up, and that it's been here all along." Tucker nodded. He looked pretty pleased with himself. "So the way I look at it, moving home is the first step, and I've taken it. I'm finally in the right place to find what I've been searching for."

Tate sank back in his chair again and recrossed is legs. "Well, now, Tuck, that's great news. But I do kind of wonder…"

"What?"

"If you don't know what it is you're searching for, how can you be sure it's here in the Junction?"

Tucker pondered that question for several long seconds. At last, he replied, "I don't know *how* I'm sure,

I just know I'm *right* to be sure. It's here. I know it is. I can feel it in my bones.''

"Ah," said Tate, since *ah* seemed like the right thing to say at that moment.

"Yeah," said Tucker. "I'm going to figure this mystery out, just you watch."

Tate shook his head. "I hope for your sake that you do—but I've gotta admit, it all sounds a little too damn deep to me."

Tucker didn't argue. "Yeah, I imagine it does."

"Anything I can do to help, you let me know."

"Thanks," Tucker said. "I will."

Tate got up and got the decanter from the liquor cart. He splashed another shot or two into both of their glasses. When he settled back into his chair and put his feet up again, he held out his glass and Tucker tapped it with his. "Whatever the reason, it's good that you're home. A man needs a place to call his own." He gave Tucker a wink. "Even if his brother holds half the deed."

"It's a big house," Tucker said helpfully.

"It damn well is," Tate agreed. By then, the brandy had him feeling relaxed and easy. He realized he was ready to talk about the exasperating woman who shared his bed. "And I guess I should bring you up to speed on what's happening with me and Molly."

"I'd appreciate that."

"Save your gratitude. It's not as though I have any real choice. You know this town. If *I* don't tell you tonight, tomorrow morning someone else will."

"Fire away."

Tate made it as short and to-the-point as possible.

"Molly's having my baby. I want her to marry me. She keeps putting me off. She's got her doubts, she says, that either of us is marriage material."

"But you did talk her into living with you?"

Tate made a scoffing sound. "Nobody talks Molly into anything. The two of us living together was her brilliant idea. She's calling it a *trial run*. Can you believe that? We're trying out being married—and after three and a half weeks of *trying,* she's still not willing to even discuss taking a chance on the real thing."

"But you're getting along all right—I mean, over-all?"

"We get along great. That is, except for the times when I ask her to marry me and she says no. Those times aren't all that terrific, if you want the truth."

Tucker swirled his brandy in the snifter, wearing the charming troublemaker's grin that always drove the ladies wild. "I've got something I want to say, but I'm afraid you might punch me out if I do."

Tate couldn't help but laugh. "The possibility of me punching you out never stopped you in the old days."

"Good point. So then I guess I'll just go for it—having first made it clear that I always thought Molly was one hell of a gal. I looked twice at her myself, back in the day, before I fell so hard for Lena Lou." When Tate glared, Tucker put up a hand, palm out. "Not that Molly ever gave *me* a look. Molly never gave *any* guy a chance, as far as I can remember. Till you, apparently…"

Tate couldn't resist remarking, "Speaking of Lena Lou."

Tucker winced. "Now, see. I knew it was a mistake to mention her name."

"She's getting married to some car salesman from over in Abilene."

"I hope she'll be very happy."

"You still got a thing for her?"

"Hell, no. That's long over—and don't think you can distract me. We're talking about you and Molly, not some girl I used to date over a decade ago." Tate grunted in a resigned sort of way. And Tucker went on, "Like I just said, I think Molly's a hell of a gal. But she's not the kind of woman I pictured you marrying. I thought for sure, when the time came, you'd hook up with someone kind of like—"

Tate said it before Tucker could. "Grandmother?"

Tucker dipped his head. "You got it."

Tate admitted, "Before Molly, I thought the same thing. But now…well, I've realized I don't want some perfect, well-bred, soft-spoken rich man's daughter for my wife. I want Molly. And she wants me, too. I just can't get her to take the leap and make it legal."

Tucker was staring at him, shaking his head.

"What?" Tate demanded in a low, threatening growl.

Tucker heaved a heavy sigh. "You poor sucker. You are gone, gone, gone."

Tate grabbed for the brandy carafe. "You better have another drink. And while you're having it, you should try to remember that this poor sucker can still kick your ass."

Tucker smiled wide then. "Same old Tate. Don't ever change."

Chapter Fourteen

It was Tate who got the bright idea to make over three of the rooms upstairs into a new master suite and nursery.

By the time he suggested the project to Molly, two weeks had passed since Tucker's return home and the sign outside Leland Hogan's law office read Hogan & Bravo, Attorneys at Law.

The August town council meeting had come and gone. Like the meeting in July, it had been pleasant and productive. And Molly's plan for indigent and shut-in care was now in place.

On the Tuesday following the meeting, Molly went to the doctor for her four-month checkup.

Her appointment was at two, and Tate was at work in his study about an hour later, when she showed up at home. He leaned back in his chair, smiling to himself, as she swore at the alarm box to the accompaniment of the piercing warning beep. She finally got it right and the beeping stopped.

By then, Miranda had come running. He heard her voice from over by the stairs. "Everything all right, Miss Molly?"

Molly made reassuring noises. Then her heels tapped his way, and a few seconds later, she stood in the open doorway, looking rounder and riper than ever. In the past couple of weeks, the baby was really starting to show.

"Hey," he said by way of greeting.

"Working hard?" Something wasn't right. Her smile tried to tease him, but didn't quite make it. It quivered at the corners.

"What's the matter?"

"Oh, Tate..." She kind of sagged against the door frame, shaking her head.

He jumped up and got around the desk and at her side in four strides. Wrapping a steadying arm around her thickening waist, he herded her toward the sitting area. "Come on. Take a load off your feet." He guided her down into one of the wing chairs. "There. Better?"

She looked up at him and frowned. "Oh, I've gotten you all worried now. Don't be. It's really nothing bad. It's only that I was so surprised, that's all."

He suggested, hopefully, "Surprised about...?"

"Tate, it's okay. You don't have to look so anxious."

"Sorry." He tried his damnedest not to look worried.

And while he was trying, she had another request.

"And will you please not loom over me like that? You're making me nervous."

He was making *her* nervous? Carefully he backed around the big ottoman and sank slowly into the other chair. "Molly."

"What?"

"How about *this?*"

"Yeah?"

"Just *tell* me what it is that you're so damn surprised about."

She gulped. "Two heartbeats."

"Two heartbeats," he repeated, more lost than ever. "And that means…?"

She threw up both hands. "Dr. Mendoza said she heard *two heartbeats.*"

He was starting to get it. "Two…you mean…?"

She was nodding. "That's right." She put her hands on her seriously burgeoning belly. "It's why I'm getting so big now. Because we're having—"

He knew then. "Twins?"

Her smile bloomed wide. "I still need an ultrasound to be absolutely certain, but Dr. Mendoza seemed pretty positive about it."

He wasn't really sure what an ultrasound was. "When?"

"The ultrasound?"

"Yeah."

"Thursday."

"Thursday." Two days away. Damn it. He wanted to know *now.*

"Oh, Tate. On Thursday, we'll know beyond a doubt. Dr. Mendoza said she couldn't understand why she didn't pick up the other heartbeat sooner. But that's how it goes. Sometimes they just can't tell for a while.''

He still couldn't quite believe it. "Twins..."

"I don't know why I'm so happy."

"Well, why the hell wouldn't you be?"

Her face got all soft and hopeful. "You like the idea then?"

He found he was grinning. "As far as I'm concerned, one's perfect. Two's two times that."

"Oh, Tate." She beamed at him, and he felt like a million bucks. "You do have your moments."

"Well, thanks. I think."

"But it's going to be a challenge, don't kid yourself it won't. Twins mean twice the work. Twice the dirty diapers, twice the nights without sleep, twice the holding and feeding and burping and Lord knows what all else."

"We'll manage. You'll see."

"Yeah," she said, all shiny-eyed. "I know we will." She sank back in the chair and chuckled. "I guess I kind of scared you, huh? I'm sorry..."

She looked so sweet and happy and...*his*. He couldn't stop himself. He sat forward, braced his elbows on his spread knees and folded his hands between them. "Damn it, Molly. Marry me. Marry me now. Our babies need that. You know that they do."

He saw the minute the words were out what her answer was going to be. He saw it in her fading smile, in the regretful frown that creased her brow.

It was the same as always.

"Oh, Tate..."

"Don't." He stood. Fast. And he told her flatly, "It's great—the twins, I mean."

She took in a shaky breath. "Well, like I said, we won't know for sure until—"

"Thursday. Got it." He gestured toward the computer waiting on his desk. "Listen, I've got a few things I'm working on here…"

"Oh. Well, yeah. I know you're busy." She pushed to her feet. "I guess I'd better get on back to the Cut, myself." She came around the ottoman for a goodbye kiss. He put his hands on her shoulders—holding her slightly away from him—and they shared a quick peck. Once their lips had met, she had the good grace to step back. "I'll, um, see you tonight, then?"

He nodded. "Tonight."

"Tate, I…"

He shook his head. "Don't."

She drew herself up nice and straight and pointed that round stomach of hers at the door. Long after he heard her pickup start up out in front, he just stood there, staring at the place where she'd been.

At dinner, Tate's brother did most of the talking. Lately Tucker was happy as a heifer with new fence post to scratch on. He and Leland got on well. He liked the view from his bedroom window. He'd hooked up with a few high school buddies and they had a running weekly poker game.

"I've been thinking," Tucker said. "I've always wanted a dog. All those years I moved around so much, it wouldn't have been right to try dragging a pet around with me. But now I'm home to stay, well, why not?"

"A dog demands a lot of care," Tate warned. And

that had him thinking, just like twins. God in heaven. *We're having* twins....

About then, Molly sent him a hopeful look. Tate pointedly turned away from her.

"I think I'm up to it," Tucker declared. "I want something big and friendly—with short hair."

"A black Lab?" Molly suggested. "They're usually sweet."

"Yeah," said Tucker. "I've been thinking maybe a Lab."

Tate tuned them out as they discussed breeds.

Why the hell wouldn't she marry him?

It was five weeks now. Count 'em. Five.

Five weeks since she moved in with him, five weeks of *playing* at being married. Five weeks of a merry-go-round of building up the nerve, asking—and getting turned down. Even a confident man could only take so much of that kind of treatment.

Deep inside, he had a secret fear. And that fear was growing stronger all the time. The fear had a voice and it whispered in his ear.

She'll never marry you. She'll dump you again. Just you wait. She'll be out of here for good one of these days and those twins she just told you about will be born without your name.

It was right then, while the fear whispered hard words in his ear and Molly and Tucker chattered on about how maybe Tucker ought to get himself a golden retriever—in spite of the longer hair, they had the perfect temperament—that the idea to fix up the rooms upstairs occurred to him.

She'd had a good time, hadn't she, getting the South Wing ready for Tucker? She really got into it,

switching out the furniture, choosing the paint, hiring
the workers and making sure they did a good job. No
reason she wouldn't enjoy making over the rooms
upstairs so they could have the baby's room—correc-
tion: *babies'* room—right next to theirs.

It was a good idea, he thought. A practical idea.
There was no room downstairs for a nursery. And she
would want to be on the same floor as the babies.

Plus, if she said yes, it would be a good sign—
wouldn't it? After all, there was no reason she would
get involved in planning a nursery if she didn't intend
to be here to see the babies use it.

He felt better, then. And when she sent him another
hopeful look, he granted her a careful smile.

Yeah, he was nervous about suggesting it to her.
What if she said no?

Well. Then he would have learned something,
wouldn't he? So what if it was something he didn't
want to know?

If she was planning on dumping him, he *needed* to
know.

He brought it up later, when they were alone. After
they'd made up, more or less. After he'd taken off all
her clothes and kissed every inch of her and pushed
her down on the pillows and buried himself inside
her. After she cried out and clung to him and they
went over the moon together.

She lay tucked up next to him, her head cradled on
his shoulder and her golden hair spilling across his
arm when he said, real casually, ''I've been thinking
that we ought to make some plans for the babies'
room....''

She didn't pull away, or stiffen up. She cuddled even closer and she tipped her head up to look at him. "What kind of plans?" She had a soft smile on her mouth and a look of interest in her eyes.

He stroked her hair. "Well, I was thinking we could move the master suite upstairs. You know the bedroom at the back, the one that used to be my mother's, with the sitting room attached?"

"The sitting room? You mean the big room with all the windows where she used to do her painting?"

"That's right, my mother's studio."

"Yeah, I'm with you." Molly's voice was eager.

He knew then that he had her, that she already liked where he was going. His confidence returned in a sweet, hot rush. "Well, you know how that bedroom at the back has the bathroom attached—and when you go through the bathroom…"

"There's that front bedroom on the other side." She canted up on an elbow—and then bent her head to plant a quick, hard kiss on his mouth. "Oh, Tate. It's a great idea. We'll have that nice bedroom and the big, bright sitting room. And the babies will be right nearby…"

He took a lock of her hair and coiled it around his index finger. "You like it?"

"I love it. I think we should start fixing it up right away."

Thursday, Molly had her ultrasound. Tate went with her. He saw his son and his daughter—faint, floating gray images on the monitor above the padded table where Molly lay. His daughter—or at least, the

one the technician *said* was his daughter—appeared
to be sucking her thumb.

"Cute, huh?" said the technician. He was moving
a wandlike device through the clear jelly he'd spread
on Molly's rounded belly.

Tate nodded, his throat clutching up and his heart
pounding fast.

Molly laughed. "You sure? A boy and a girl? How
can you tell?"

The technician pointed out what was apparently the
crucial evidence. Molly nodded. "Ah…"

Tate only stared. In the strange, black and white
pulsing space on the monitor, things weren't all that
clear.

Not that it really mattered. As he'd become more
accustomed to the idea of being a father, he'd cared
less and less whether their child was a boy or girl.
And now that there were *two* children, well…

Twin sons. Twin daughters. One of each.

It had somehow become fine with him, whichever
they were. Just let them be healthy, he thought.
Healthy and strong. And Tate would be satisfied.

Saturday, Molly woke early with a feeling of anticipation. A skinny shaft of bright Texas sun found
its way in at the split in the curtains. It was going to
be a hot one, according to yesterday's weather report.

102…in the shade.

Not that it mattered how hot it was going to be out
there. It was cool in the ranch house and Molly was
planning on going nowhere that day. Yesterday, she'd
managed to reschedule all her appointments. She had
today to herself. And Sunday and Monday were her

usual days off. She might check in at the salon Monday, just to see how things were going and pick up the deposit to take to the bank, but essentially, she would have a three-day weekend to get going on the rooms upstairs.

She smiled at the sleeping man beside her. A dark lock of shiny hair had fallen half-across his forehead. Molly resisted the urge to smooth it back.

He looked so peaceful and sweet when he was sleeping. She didn't want to disturb him. She just wanted to lie there for a moment and enjoy the sight of him with his mouth all soft and his eyelashes so long and spiky against his tanned cheeks.

They were doing real well, she thought. Day-by-day she was growing more and more certain that they had a chance together—and a pretty good one, too.

Soon, she was going to tell him that she would be proud to be his wife. Heck. Maybe she should have said yes the other day, in his study, when she broke the news to him about the twins.

But it was so strange. Every time he asked her, she would look at him and her chest would feel tight. She would think how much she wanted him, how she couldn't picture her life anymore without him in it.

And still, at that moment, the moment when he asked her, she just couldn't do it—couldn't open her mouth and say the word "yes."

She wanted him—wanted to *be* with him. But at the same time there was a painful and powerful conflicting feeling that something was missing.

That something just wasn't right.

She'd tried more than once to explain it to him. But what was there to explain, really?

It was nothing concrete. She had no real *reason* to keep telling him no.

And he was getting pretty put out about it. Each time he asked and she turned him down, it took him a little bit longer to forgive her.

And really, could she blame him?

She was carrying his babies. He treated her right, and they had a great life together.

What more was there for her to want before she could say yes?

Molly didn't rightly know.

She wondered sometimes if there was something really *wrong* with her. Maybe all those years of Granny's man-bashing, maybe the fact that her own dad had run off without even telling her mom his name. Maybe the bad treatment Dixie later received at the hands of too many mean men...

Maybe all that had gotten to her, to Molly. Maybe it had shaped her somehow, messed her up in a permanent way. Maybe she was never going to get past her upbringing to become the kind of woman who could hook up long-term with a man.

Times like this, when she looked at Tate sleeping beside her and she realized deep in her heart that he was all she wanted in the world—he, and their babies. Times like this, she couldn't help wondering what the heck was the matter with her.

She couldn't resist. She reached out and pushed that fallen lock of hair back from his forehead.

His eyes opened and gave her a slow, lazy kind of smile. "C'mere." He hooked his big arm around her and gathered her close.

Soon, she thought, as she turned and cuddled

against him, spoon-fashion. *Soon, I will manage to tell him yes....*

After breakfast, Tate had to head into town for meetings with two of his partners—Davey Luster at the hardware store and Morley Pribble at the Gas 'n Go. Molly commandeered Miranda and Jesse and they went to work upstairs.

The first order of business was to clear out Penelope's studio. Tate had said Molly could put everything in a storage room off the old barn behind the back gardens until they had a chance to go through it and decide what to keep. So she and Miranda packed boxes, and Jesse carted it all down the stairs and out to the barn.

It was kind of sad, really, putting away all the stuff that Penelope would never use again, including a few unfinished paintings—of the view out the window on the garden in back; of Tucker, taken from an old childhood photograph clipped to the edge of the canvas; of a scary-looking fellow with wolflike silver-gray eyes.

It was not only that Penelope was gone from this life, but also the very *badness* of the paintings that made the job of packing away her studio more than a little bit depressing. Molly was no expert on fine art, but even she could see that Penelope Tate Bravo had possessed almost no artistic talent. Maybe Penelope should have tried those kinds of paintings with just splashes of color all over the place and nothing recognizable, nothing from the real world. If she had, it would have been harder for your average, everyday person to figure out how terrible her paintings were.

But instead, Penelope had painted people and places that were supposed to look like real life. So the bench in the back garden was flat-looking, like nothing anyone could ever sit on, and Tucker came out with a head shaped like a pinto bean. And that strange, evil-looking guy with the silver eyes—well, nobody had eyes like that, now did they?

And Penelope had kept at it all her life. Now, why, Molly wondered, did that seem so sad? After all, people did have hobbies, didn't they? There was no law that said you had to be good at something you did for pleasure—was there?

Maybe it was just all the stories Molly had heard. About poor, beaten-down Penelope, dominated for most of her life by her man's man of a father, Ol' Tuck, only escaping him just long enough to get pregnant by a stranger—twice. Ol' Tuck, folks said, had as good as taken her boys from her. He'd brought them up the way he though they should be raised. The only thing she'd really had was her painting— and she wasn't any good at that.

By noon, when they broke for lunch, Molly had the studio pretty much handled. With the clutter of easels and canvases and all the paint supplies cleared out, the beauty of the big, sunny room came all the clearer. The parquet floor, paint-spattered and scratched, needed stripping and waxing. And the walls cried out for fresh paint—a leaf-green or a honey tan, she was thinking, with the woodwork all in fresh, clean white. She'd see to all that during the week. And she would get Tate out with her next weekend to choose some furniture. They could drive into Abilene, make a day of it. And before that, she would check in the storage areas around the property to see if anything they already had would look good up here.

Tate came home and joined her for lunch in the breakfast room. She brought him up to speed on her progress upstairs, and he told her about how Ray and Davey Luster were getting along.

"Davey's kind of fussy," Tate said. "And Ray takes things slow and easy. I swear, it's beginning to seem like Ray is settling Davey down—and Davey's teaching Ray to be responsible."

She looked across the table at him and thought again about saying yes, about just popping out with it, right there, over taco salads and lemonade.

Tate. We really are working out just fine together. I would be so pleased and happy if we could get married right away....

But the minutes ticked past and they ate the salad from their taco shells and drank their lemonade and somehow, by the time he got up to head on over to the Cottonwood Room at the country club for a few games of pool with a couple of his rich friends, she still hadn't said the magic words.

He bent over her chair and she tipped her head back and they kissed, a sweet, long kiss that curled her toes and made her heart beat faster. When he pulled away, he asked, "You sure you don't need my help upstairs?" His big hand rested on her shoulder.

She gave that hand a fond pat. "Go on, meet your friends."

"How about in a few hours, I come back and get you? You can drive out to the airfield with me and we can—"

She shook her head before he could go any further.

"No way. I'm not getting near that airfield any time soon. You know the minute I do, Granny'll start in on me to go flying with her."

He squeezed her shoulder. "Truth is, I was thinking of trying to get you up in the air myself."

"Later for that."

He chuckled. "When's later?"

"Not while I'm pregnant, I can promise you that much—but you go ahead. And maybe tomorrow, after church, you can help me out some upstairs."

He bent close for one more kiss—a quick one, that time—and then he was gone. She lingered alone at the table for a few minutes, sipping her lemonade, wondering again why she never could manage to get the important words out.

Upstairs, Molly started on Penelope's bedroom. She was clearing out the big mahogany bureau, putting Penelope's socks and sweaters and lingerie into boxes, when Miranda and Jesse appeared in the doorway to the hall. She sent them back to their regular duties. Tomorrow, after she'd filled a bunch of boxes, the housekeeper and her husband could start carrying things downstairs.

Once the bureau was empty, she tackled the closet, which smelled faintly of paint thinner and Chanel No. 5. Molly folded up and boxed the dresses and skirts and blouses and three racks of expensive shoes—some, judging by the style of them, over twenty years old.

Once she got the clothes and the shoes out, she had only the stacks of boxes on the upper shelves to deal with. There were a lot of those, of varying sizes. Some contained purses and some, more shoes. Some held books. A couple were filled with photographs. Molly took a half hour or so to glance through those, smiling at the occasional pictures of Tate and Tucker as they were growing up, studying the stern face and tall, broad-shouldered figure of Tucker Tate IV and the delicate form of Tate's grandmother.

Finally she put the boxes of pictures aside. She could spend forever going through them. But if she did that right now, she wouldn't achieve her goal of getting the bedroom packed up by dinnertime.

She'd reached the end of the shelf on one side, and was taking down the last box there when the floor beneath her feet gave an odd, rubbing kind of squeak. If she hadn't had that secret compartment in her bedroom closet at home, she probably wouldn't have given the faint squeaky noise a second thought.

But she did have a hidey-hole at home. She knew that if you stood on it just right you'd get a sound like the one she'd just heard.

Molly left that final box on the end of the shelf and knelt to have a look. The overhead light wasn't all that bright, and her body cast a shadow, but since she knew right where to look, she quickly found the secret compartment by feel. The hooked-together section of boards pried up easily.

Underneath, she could see…a book. Hardbound, dark green, it looked like, with a gold border in a pattern of leaves and flowers. The gold leaf shone dully when it caught the dim overhead light. Beneath the book was a fat manila envelope.

She started to reach for the book, but thought better of that. A dark, undisturbed hole in the floor was a prime hiding place for fiddleback spiders and who knew what other kinds of biting, dangerous critters.

She levered to her heels and then rose to her feet and went out into the bedroom to get the flashlight she'd left on the bureau. Back on her knees in the closet, she shone the light into the shadowed space.

No spiders or other creepy creatures that she could see. Since the book was on top, she reached in and snatched it out. She blew the dust off the gold-trimmed cover and opened it.

The first page was blank, except for the words *Penelope Tate Bravo* and a date—almost three years ago—written in a cramped, back-slanted hand. Some kind of journal, then?

Molly began flipping through the gold-leafed pages. They were all filled with writing in that same tortured hand.

Tate's mother's journal…

Oh, my, my. This was just too exciting!

Carefully, watching for anything that might bite, she reached into the secret space a second time and pulled out the thick manila envelope. A quick final scan with the flashlight and she was sure that was it. Nothing else in there.

Her goal to get the bedroom packed up in the next couple of hours forgotten, Molly took the book and the envelope out of the closet and set them on the bed. As she stood looking down at them, she wondered if she ought to wait to start nosing through them until Tate got home. After all, they *were* his mother's private papers.

And there must be secrets involved—or why would

they have been stashed in a hidden compartment in the back of the closet?

She glanced at the clock by the bed. It would be at least a couple of hours before Tate returned....

Maybe just a tiny peek.

She opened the curtains wide to let in the afternoon sun, slipped off her shoes and climbed up on the bed. She took a minute to plump the pillows. Then, with an eager sigh of pure anticipation, she opened the manila envelope and peered inside.

Newspaper clippings.

Carefully she reached in and scooped them out onto the floral-patterned bedspread. There were at least twenty of them, some dated as recently as three years ago—some over thirty years old.

They concerned a man named Blake Bravo and the wealthy Southern California family that had disowned him. They recorded Blake Bravo's death by fire—at just about the time that Tate's father would have died—and the kidnapping of the deceased Blake's baby nephew, Russell Bravo, the famous Bravo Baby, two years later.

There was a picture of Blake as a very young man, in a family portrait with his mother and father and brother, Jonas. Those silver eyes were unmistakable. They were the eyes in Penelope's unfinished painting. So strange, Molly thought. Despite being such a bad artist, she'd managed to get those eyes right.

And what could all this mean, but that the silver-eyed Blake Bravo had been Penelope's lost husband—and Tate's father?

In the more recent clippings, it came to light that Blake Bravo had actually lived another thirty-two years after he was supposed to have been dead and buried. As Molly already knew, the long-missing Bravo Baby was finally found living in Oklahoma City, a grown man who had no idea of his original identity. It had been Blake—dead for real, at last, of heart disease—who had kidnapped him all those years and years before.

Molly sat for a while, staring at the yellowed clippings spread out on the bed beside her.

It had just never occurred to her that those legendary Los Angeles Bravos could have a thing to do with Tate. She doubted anyone else in town had made the connection, either. If they had, you could be darn sure it would have spread through the Junction like a grassfire in a high wind.

And speaking of who knew, what about Tate? Was it possible that *he* knew who his father really was?

Uh-uh. Unlikely. From the few brief talks they'd had on the subject, Molly was pretty certain that Tate really believed his father had died all those years ago, before Tate was even born. Tate surely knew his father's first name—though, now she thought about it, he'd never mentioned it to her. But apparently, even if he knew that his father had been a man named Blake Bravo, he'd never connected him up with the notorious kidnapper of the Bravo Baby.

And wait a minute.

If Tate's dad didn't really die until three years ago, then it *would* have been possible for him to be Tucker's dad, too.

She scanned the clippings again. Yes! Norman, Oklahoma. Blake Bravo had lived there, keeping a low profile for thirty years, and never been caught out until he died and his son went through his effects.

Molly blinked. *His son.* Blake Bravo had a son by his *wife* in Norman, Oklahoma.

A kidnapper. A bigamist. And Lord knew what-all else. From what the clippings revealed, Blake Bravo had not, in any sense, been a nice man.

And the University of Oklahoma was in Norman. And the OU-Texas rivalry was a long-standing one. That Blake might have attended a certain OU-Texas game three decades ago wasn't all that hard to imagine. It was definitely possible that Penelope had run into her "dead" husband there.

Eager to fill in the gaps in the story, Molly picked up the journal and started to read.

It began, *This book is for my sons, Tate and Tucker Bravo. It is my hope that, after reading what I write here and seeing the evidence in the envelope that accompanies it, they will understand the story of how they came to be....*

Chapter Fifteen

After a pleasant three hours of playing eight ball at the club, Tate drove out to the airfield, where he took Dusty up in the Cessna—or rather, Dusty took him.

She finally had her private license and that woman was ready to get in the pilot's seat. Altogether, it was a pretty smooth flight. As soon as the twins were born, Tate decided, he would help Dusty convince Molly to let her granny take her up.

He got back to the ranch house at a little after five and headed straight for the shower to wash off the airfield dust. Twenty minutes later, in clean cargoes and a fresh shirt, he found Miranda in the kitchen and learned that Molly had gone upstairs after lunch and hadn't come back down yet.

So he climbed the stairs, patting himself on the back the whole way for coming up with the idea to change the rooms around. Molly had jumped on it like a duck on a june bug. It was a good sign, wasn't it, that she got right into making a place for them— together—*and* for their babies? She would have them moved upstairs and the nursery ready in no time— and maybe, the next time he popped the question, she would finally say yes.

He found her propped against the headboard on his mother's bed, a book open on her lap and yellowed bits of newsprint spread out beside her. She glanced up as he entered, her eyes agleam, a big smile on her mouth and a smudge of dust on her nose.

"Tate. Come here. Sit down…" She put the book on her other side and quickly scooped up the news-paper clippings into a big envelope she grabbed from the nightstand.

He took the place she'd cleared for him. "Getting in a little reading?"

"Oh, Tate…" She looked breathless. Thrilled.

About what? A book and some old newspaper clip-pings?

Affectionately, he rubbed away the smudge of dirt on her nose. "I see you've made some serious prog-ress." There were boxes stacked by the bureau and several more beside the closet door.

"Yeah. It's going great. But, Tate…" She grabbed his hand, kissed the back of it. "Oh, my golly. I just don't know where to begin."

He sat back a little. "About…?"

"This," she announced, grabbing the gold-trimmed green book and waving it at him. "And these!" She dropped the book and waved the enve-lope full of the clippings she'd gathered up from the bed. "These were your mother's. I found them, under the floorboards in the back of the closet."

"Okay," he said cautiously.

"Tate, she meant for you to have them, but I guess she never got around to giving them to you before she got hit by that semitruck. Or, I don't know, maybe she could never quite get up the nerve." Molly was pretty nigh on bouncing in place, her face flushed, her eyes wide with excitement. "Tate, you remember the Bravo Baby, don't you?"

He wasn't getting this. "Yeah. So?"

"Well…oh, Tate. He's…well, he would be your cousin, I think."

He sat back from her even farther. "What the hell are you talking about?"

"The Bravo Baby, he's your—" She cut herself off. "Oh, I don't think I'm going about this right. I, well, I don't even know where to start…"

"Just try the beginning," he said. "Just start from there."

So she did, eagerly, her eyes shining, laying out an outrageous story of how his father hadn't really died thirty-five years ago, after all. Instead he'd faked his own death in an apartment fire—to escape a manslaughter conviction, Molly said. "Or at least, he was up on a manslaughter charge before he pretended to get dead. He'd beat some poor guy to death in a brawl." It went on like that, getting worse and worse. His father had kidnapped the Bravo Baby, she said— and the famous Los Angeles Bravos were Tate's own relatives. "And Tucker actually *is* Blake Bravo's son, just like you are," she said. "Your mother ran off with Blake for a second time, spotted him at an OU-

Texas game, just like she always claimed—spotted him and ran off with him right there and then. He was her grand passion, you know? She couldn't resist him. But then he got bored with her and left her sleeping in their motel room—just vanished into the darkness. She had to come crawling back to your mean grand-daddy.'' She waved the book at him. ''It says so right in here. And Tate, Blake Bravo was *married* to some-one else—after your mother. And he had a son by her. You've got a half brother up there in Norman, Oklahoma. And your father told her he had sons and a wife in Nevada, too—and a couple of other states he didn't name. Your mother writes in here that she thinks your father was capable of just about anything. But, see, when she was young, she didn't even care. When he crooked his little finger, she came running. She put it down in this book that she'd figured out a lot of stuff about him after that first time he was sup-posed to have died. It was in all the papers and she saw the pictures of him and she knew it was the man she had married.''

Why was she telling him this? Did she really be-lieve he cared to know that his father was a crook and a thief and a murderer? Did she really imagine that it was true?

It wasn't, of course. He refused to believe it. His father had died over three decades ago. He'd been an honest man who married his mother—and *only* his mother.

She wasn't finished. ''Tate, that first time your mother came home, before you were born, after Blake had supposedly died, she *told* your granddaddy ev-erything she knew. And your granddaddy made her swear to keep her mouth shut about it, to give you your daddy's name, since she did have a marriage license, and just tell folks your daddy had died and nothing else about him. Your mother writes that she doesn't even think your granddaddy believed her about your father. Your granddaddy thought she made it all up, that she was 'sensitive' and given to 'wild imaginings' and—''

He'd heard enough. ''Because she was.''

Molly blinked. ''Well, maybe. I don't know. But—''

''That's right. You don't know. You don't know a damn thing about my mother—or my father. You dig some newspaper clippings and a diary out of a hole in the floor and you plunk yourself down and you read it all through, even though it might be something that's none of your business.''

''No. Tate. Wait a minute…'' She paused, looking sheepish. ''Okay, I probably shouldn't have—''

''You're right, you shouldn't have. But that's not the point, so we'll let that go.'' He picked up the envelope from where she'd dropped it on the bed. ''And give me that damn book.''

''Tate, I don't—''

''Just give it here, Molly. Give it here, now.'' Looking wide-eyed and worried, she handed it over. ''Now. Where'd you say you found these?''

''In the closet. In the back, in a hole in the floor.''

He got up and tossed both things—the damn book and the envelope—in the trash basket next to the bureau. ''Well, now they're in the garbage. We don't ever have to speak of them—or even think about them—anymore.''

She leapt off the bed. "What are you talking about? It's…well, it's the truth, Tate. The truth about who you are and who your family is. About your father." She stood in the middle of the floor and she raked her blond hair back off of her forehead and let out a small, pained kind of sound. "I don't get it. I'd give just about anything to know something about *my* father."

He tried to be patient with her. "It's not true. None of it. My mother lived in her own little world. She made it all up, that's all. It's not—"

She cut him off. "Look. Will you please just read it? Will you look at the clippings and—"

"Why? What will a bunch of old clippings prove? Sure, there was a Bravo Baby. Everyone knows that. But just because he had the same last name as I do doesn't make him my cousin. Just because my father's name was Blake doesn't mean he was *that* Blake. Can't you see? It's all just…made up."

"You don't know that. It could just as likely be true. And it wouldn't take all that much of an effort to contact the Bravo family in Los Angeles—or the half brother you very well might have in Oklahoma."

"That's about the damn dumbest idea you ever had. Why would I want to go contacting some man I don't even know to find out if he's my brother? He's *not* my brother."

"Marsh," she said, as if that was supposed to mean something to him. "His name is Marsh Bravo, your half brother in Oklahoma. You know he wouldn't be that hard to find." She got right up in his face about it.

He took her by the shoulders and gave her a shake.

"Molly, listen. I don't want to find him. I know who I am, and I don't need to go running off half-cocked because of some crazy stuff my mother wrote in a diary."

She stared up at him, wearing a look of bewildered amazement. "But, Tate. If you'll only look at the clippings, read what she wrote…"

"No."

"But—"

"Molly, I said no. I don't care what she wrote. It doesn't matter. It's all just made up. Some kind of fantasy. That's how my mother was."

She shook off his grip. "How do you know that? I mean, did you ever even really *know* her? Did you ever even give her half a chance?" She backed away from him. "It bothers me, Tate. I have to tell you, it really does, that you could disrespect your own mother in this way."

"What's disrespectful? My mother had a tendency to live in a fantasy world. That's a fact."

"Fact? What are you talking about? It's a fact that she painted really terrible paintings. It's a fact that your granddaddy ran her and your grandmother and pretty much everything else in this town. It's a fact that he treated her like a second-class citizen, a fact that she wasn't even allowed to raise her own sons. But who says your mother lived in a fantasy world?" She put out a hand and then slapped her thigh with it. "No. No, wait. Don't tell me. I'll bet your mean old granddaddy did. And you believed him." It was an accusation.

He refused to be accused. "Damn straight, I believed him. I knew my own mother—which you did not. I believed what my grandfather said about her because it was *true*."

Molly was shaking her head. "Oh, Tate. How can you talk about truth when you're so busy hiding from it? You won't even give the truth half a chance. You've got it stuck in your head that you're okay and I'm not—or Tucker, either, for that matter. You got some big thing about how your mom and dad were married and he died, all innocent and simple and aboveboard, and that's the way it is, that's the way it *has* to be. Even though you know damn well that the story you've been living by doesn't really add up."

"What the hell? Yeah, it adds up. It adds up better than this crazy load of bull you're trying to hand me."

"No. No, it doesn't. Oh, please, won't you just read what—"

He chopped the air with a sweep of his arm. "Enough. That junk is in the trash and that is where it stays."

"Will you just listen to yourself? You know who you sound like? Like your granddaddy, that's who."

"How the hell would you know that? You didn't know my grandfather. I'll bet you never exchanged two words with the man."

"No, I didn't. I didn't need to. After all, I know *you*—and if you won't take a look at that book and those clippings for your own sake, then what about Tucker, huh? Doesn't he have a right to read what his own mother wrote?"

"Tucker doesn't need to—"

She didn't let him finish. "How do you know what Tucker needs? If you would just open that book and look at the beginning, you will see that your mother wrote that book for *both* of you, to explain how you both came to be. Maybe you don't care about the truth, but Tucker just might feel differently.''

''It's not the truth. He doesn't need to know about it.''

''Oh, now.'' She spoke through clenched teeth, shaking her head. ''Now, *that* is crazy. Oh, what is the matter with you? You are just so…screwed up when it comes to this.''

That did it. Inside Tate, something went *snap*. ''*I'm* screwed up?''

Molly drew herself up and braced her hands on her hips. ''Well, yeah. Yeah, you are. About this, you are.''

Who the hell was she to tell him *he* was screwed up? ''And what about you, Molly? What about you? You have been running me around for over a month now, turning me down every time I dare to ask you if, maybe, just possibly, you might be ready to consider doing me the *honor* of being my wife. You're willing to live here, to sleep in my bed with me. Oh, yeah. You're more than happy to play house. But the real thing? Uh-uh. You won't go there. What the hell is that all about? You like to keep a man dangling, is that it? You like to put him off and shake your head and never quite be ready to take the big step? Until you got a guy so beaten down he doesn't even remember the time when he used to be something resembling a man. Is that what you like, Molly? Is that what you're all about?''

''No,'' she said, her mouth suddenly slack, her brows drawn in. ''No, that's not so. I only—''

He put up a hand. ''You know what? I don't want

to hear it. I don't want any more of your damn excuses. I don't want to be put off one more damn time. I'm asking you right now, Molly, and it's the last time I'll ever ask. So, for the moment, you'd better forget my mother and her crazy delusions. Forget the family you *think* I've got. Let's get down to what matters here. Let's get down to you and me and our babies that need us. Let's get down to the big question just one more time.''

Now she had a look as if he'd hauled off and hit her. ''Oh, Tate…don't…''

But it was too late to stop. Too late to call himself back from the brink. This thing with the diary and the envelope full of clippings had gotten to him, and gotten to him good. It had brought his frustration and simmering anger at Molly to a quick, rolling boil.

She had him tied in knots, and that was a damn fact. He'd been frustrated for too long now and his frustration kept growing. He hated not knowing— would she stay? Or would she go?

It made him feel less than a man, the way she kept him dangling. And he wasn't putting up with it any damn longer. ''You can give me a yes, and we'll get married, like we should have done weeks ago. Or you can forget it. You can pack up your stuff and move out of my house.''

She sank to the edge of his mother's bed. ''Oh, Tate…''

''Damn you, Molly. Just say it. Will you marry me, or not?''

''Please don't—''

"*Now,* Molly. Give me an answer now."

She looked at him for the longest time. And then, very softly, she whispered, "No. I can't marry you, Tate. Not now. Not like this."

Chapter Sixteen

An hour after Tate delivered his ultimatum, Molly climbed the steps to her own little house.

When she pushed the door open, Granny gasped. "Sugar pie, what are you doing here?" Granny sat on the couch with Skinny. They had the trays set up and were eating fried chicken and biscuits as they watched some old Western on TV.

"Sorry to cramp your style, Granny, but I'm moving back in."

Granny picked up the remote and muted the sound just as Andy Devine rode in on a mule. "Aw, honey. You're leaving Tate?"

Molly gulped to keep from bursting into tears. "'Fraid so."

Skinny pushed his tray aside and stood. "You got more than that suitcase there to bring in?"

Molly nodded. Without another word, Skinny went out to get the rest of her things.

"Oh, baby love…" Granny had pushed her own tray away, too. She was on her feet, skinny arms outstretched. With a cry, Molly dropped her suitcase and flung herself into her granny's embrace. Granny held her good and tight. She whispered the things a good granny always says. "Now, now. I'm here. I've got you. Nothing's ever so bad it can't be made right…"

Molly's throat closed up and her eyes started to burn. "He drew the line on me," she whispered raggedly against her granny's wrinkled neck. "He said I had to marry him, or move out."

Granny hugged her harder and clucked her tongue. "That man. What a darn fool."

"I just…I couldn't say yes, you know?"

"Well, of course you couldn't. What self-respecting woman is gonna say yes when she's forced into it?"

"No. See, what I mean is, I never *could* say yes. Even before—when we were getting along so well—even then, when he'd asked, I couldn't quite make myself tell him I'd marry him. Oh, Granny. I just…he's the only man I ever wanted. And still, I never could quite say yes. Something must be wrong with me, don't you think?"

"Nothing's wrong with you that's not wrong with half the people in this country," declared Granny. "You just give the both of you a little time and space. Things'll work themselves out, you watch and see."

"Oh, I don't know…"

Granny patted her back and stroked her hair. "Things'll work out, they will. You'll see." Granny took her by the shoulders and held her away enough that their eyes could meet. "It ain't over till it's over—and that will only be when the both of you are dead."

Molly sniffed. "Is that supposed to reassure me?"

Granny sighed. "You listen, now. Skinny'll bring in the rest of your clothes and put them in your bedroom. You don't have to worry about a thing right this minute besides washing up and sitting yourself down for some chicken and biscuits. Nothing like a good meal in your belly to lift your spirits when you're feeling low."

Tate sat down to dinner at seven—alone. Tucker wasn't home yet from wherever he'd got himself off to that day. And Molly?

Tate picked up his napkin and snapped it open so hard it sounded like a .22 going off right there in the dining room.

Molly didn't live there anymore.

Tate smoothed his napkin on his lap and picked up his fork. He'd done the right thing, and no one would dare to say he hadn't. She was never going to marry him, and it was better if he just got used to the idea, better if he stopped letting her string him along.

He was a man, wasn't he? And a man can only take so much of being denied.

His babies...

He cleared his throat—loudly—and stabbed at a piece of carrot.

His babies would be born without his name. So be it. He didn't like it. He would never like it. It was wrong. But he was through lying to himself that Molly would ever do the right thing and marry him.

Once they *were* born, well, he'd have to see about what to do next. Maybe they'd be better off full-time with him. Yeah. Maybe he would have to take his children away from her.

For their own good, of course, whispered a voice in his head that sounded suspiciously like his grandfather's.

Tate sat very still. *No,* he thought. *I am not like my grandfather, no matter what anybody says. I'm my own damn man, and I'll decide what to do about the children later.* There would be plenty of time for that.

Right now, he only had to...

What?

He looked down at the slice of carrot on the end of his fork and muttered aloud, "Eat, damn it." He poked the carrot in his mouth and stolidly chewed.

It tasted like sawdust.

He put down his fork. He had no appetite. No point in eating when he wasn't the least bit hungry.

Tate tucked his napkin in at the side of his plate and pushed back his chair. *Work,* he thought. He always had plenty of that to do.

An hour later, as he sat at his desk, staring blindly at the computer screen and scrolling randomly up and down the rows of figures before him, he heard an eager, whining sound coming from the doorway.

He glanced that way. The ugliest puppy he'd ever seen—with wiry hair and short legs and enormous feet—sat there watching him. When he looked at it, it stood up on those ridiculous stumpy legs and wagged its skinny wire-haired tail.

"Tucker," he said darkly.

Laughing, Tucker appeared in the doorway and scooped up the ugly little mutt, which immediately wiggled in ecstasy and licked him repeatedly on the face. "Meet Fargo," he said, dodging that big, wet puppy tongue.

"What is it?" Tate asked, against his own better judgment.

"Good question," said his brother, scratching the ugly thing behind one of its floppy ears. The dog whimpered in ecstasy. Tucker held it away and studied it for a moment. "My guess? Wired-haired terrier of one kind or other and maybe dachshund or beagle."

"Damn, Tuck. It's a mess."

Tucker pulled the puppy close and covered its big ears. "Don't listen, Fargo. He doesn't mean it."

"The hell I don't—and don't tell me you're keeping it."

"I'm keeping it," Tucker told him, wearing a wide grin, scratching the thing under its chin.

"I thought you were talking about a black Lab, or a golden retriever?"

"Now, what do I need with some big, noble, gorgeous pedigreed dog? Uh-uh. Fargo's more my style. I knew it the minute I spotted him, on my way home just now. He was waiting outside the Gas 'n Go, in a big box labeled Free Puppies."

"Well. At least you didn't pay good money for it."

Tucker hoisted the puppy up on his shoulder where it promptly set to work licking his ear. "Enough with insulting my dog," he said, half joking. But half not.

"Yeah, yeah. Whatever you say." Tate couldn't help asking, "Why Fargo?"

Tucker shrugged. "Why not? You want to hold him?"

"Ah. No."

"Where's Molly? She's gonna love him."

Molly.

For a moment there, while he ribbed his brother about his rotten taste in dogs, he'd almost succeeded in pushing her from his mind.

But now she was back. With a vengeance. His gut tightened and he wanted to break something.

Tucker was frowning. "Tate?"

Might as well say it. It wasn't as if Tuck wouldn't find out soon enough. "Molly's gone."

Tucker said nothing. He put the dog down. It set off, wiggling around the room, sniffing the furniture.

"That dog had better not—"

"He's newspaper-trained, and he used the Classifieds about ten minutes ago. Molly's gone where?"

"Home."

"But this *is* her ho…" Tucker's voice trailed off and his mouth fell open. "You didn't."

Tate had a powerful urge to pick up his computer monitor and hurl it against the far wall. Instead, he said, very carefully, "I didn't what?"

"Send her away…" Tucker looked at him narrowly. "By God. You did. She's the best thing that ever happened to you, and *you* went and sent her away."

"You don't know squat. And that's just fine. Because all you *need* to know is that she's moved out. She won't be coming back."

That should have been enough information for Tucker, shouldn't it?

"Why?"

Tate just looked at him, for a long time. He was waiting for his brother to give up and go away.

But Tucker didn't give up. And he didn't go anywhere, either. He stayed in the doorway, looking grim. "Tate, I asked you why?"

"Why?" repeated Tate, dangerously soft and low. "You want to know *why?*"

"That's right. I do."

Tate laid it on him. "Because she told me *no* one too many times, that's why. Because she had to nose around where she had no business going—and then she wouldn't give it up when I told her to let it be."

Tucker's dog had wandered back to him. It plopped to its haunches and looked up at its master with a small, hopeful whine. Tucker bent again and scooped it up. That time, the puppy didn't squirm or try to lick Tucker's face. It just hung there, cupped in Tucker's hand, draped along his arm. It had its tongue hanging out and it panted, happy as a pig in a pen full of manure.

"Give what up?" Tucker asked.

Tate was getting good and tired of answering Tucker's questions. At the same time, far back in his mind somewhere, a tiny voice that just might have been his conscience nagged, *If you didn't want him asking about the damn diary and those old newspaper clippings, you shouldn't have made mention of her nosing around in them, now should you?*

"Tate?" Tucker asked. Tate growled in response. Tucker demanded, "What the hell is going on?"

About then, something Molly had said started playing through Tate's mind.

Maybe you don't care about the truth, but Tucker just might feel differently....

Damn it. All right. It *was* possible that she had a point there—or at least a half of one.

Tate still believed that the diary contained nothing more than a lonely, fanciful woman's absurd imaginings. But that woman was Tucker's mother, too. Tucker did have a right to make his own decision about whether to read it or not.

Tate stood. He came around the desk and strode to the door, which his brother was blocking. "Step aside."

There was one of those moments. Tucker looked at Tate and Tate glared back at him. Tate was thinking he wouldn't mind a fight in the least. Beating up his brother and breaking some furniture might take the edge off what was eating him. He had a sense Tucker was just irritated enough at him to throw the first punch.

But in the end, Tucker stepped back into the entry hall, clearing the doorway. Tate went through. "This way," he said over his shoulder as he headed for the stairs.

Tucker fell in behind him. Tate mounted the stairs, his brother's footsteps echoing behind his own. At the upstairs landing, he led Tucker around to the half-packed-up room that had once been their mother's.

"Wow," Tucker said. "Haven't been up here since I got back..." His dog gave a whimper and Tucker petted it, soothing it.

Tate bent down and picked up the trash basket on

the far side of the bureau. He shoved it at Tucker. "Here."

"Great. Now you want me to take out the trash."

With a heavy sigh, Tate pulled out the envelope of clippings and the gold-trimmed green book and put the trash basket back on the floor. "These were our mother's. Some sort of diary and a bunch of clippings from old newspapers. Molly found them in a hidden compartment in the back of the closet."

"Hidden? Why?"

"You want to take a guess at how many times you've said 'why' in the last ten minutes?"

"But I don't—"

"Look. You want answers?" He shoved the stuff at Tucker again. That time Tucker took it. "Start reading."

Somehow, by Tuesday, when Molly went back to work, everyone in town seemed to know that she wasn't living with Tate anymore.

"Molly, you don't need that man. It's a good thing you got out from under his thumb."

"Now, Molly, you should go back, don't you think? Whatever happened between the two of you, it can be patched up."

"You got a pair of buns in the oven, hon. And than means you are in serious need of a ring on your finger. When you gonna realize that?"

"It's a woman's place to crawl sometimes. Don't take it personal. Just get down on your knees and beg him to forgive you for whatever it was he says you did..."

"Darlin', you are free at last. I knew you'd get

away from him. And I don't care what the rest of them say. I say, good for you..."

How did they find out so fast? Molly wondered. Tate wouldn't have said anything—or anyone in her family. Or Tucker, either, though she imagined he must have known by then.

Maybe Miranda or Jesse?

But both of them had known what she and Tate were up to in March, during their three weeks of secret passion. They had never said a word to anyone. It made no sense they'd be spreading tales now.

So who had spilled the beans?

Molly figured she'd probably never know. Living in the Junction, you just had to accept that any secret you had wouldn't stay that way for long.

And that everyone knew she and Tate were over hardly mattered to her, anyway. She went through each day in a fog of longing and sadness. She missed Tate *so* much. It was like what they say will happen when you lose an arm. You still feel as if it's there. Every now and then, you completely forget that one of your arms is gone.

And then you look over—what the heck? Nothing there.

Like that. A ghost arm—her ghost love. Tate was there, in her heart. If she never saw him again, it wouldn't matter. He was never going to go away.

Granny tried to tease her out of her misery. "Get me my shotgun, lovey dear. That Tate'll come back to you—or I'll blow a hole in him."

Dixie tried to get her to go talk to him. "Go to him, baby. You can work it out, I know you can."

Dixie just didn't understand. Tate had delivered the

ultimatum, and Molly had refused to do what he wanted and now there was no fixing things, no making things right. Not with a man like Tate.

In her sadness, she often pondered the fact that Tate's very strength and purposefulness and uncompromising nature were what had made him the only man she'd ever looked twice at. Really, they were so very much alike, the two of them.

Maybe *too* much alike.

Yeah. To make it work between a man and a woman, one of them had to give in now and then. Molly hadn't, and Tate wouldn't.

Where did that leave them?

Separated. With the whole dang town talking about it.

"And you're having twins, too," Donetta said.

Molly scowled at Donetta in the styling station mirror. "How did you know that?"

"Well, honey. Don't you remember? You told everyone last week."

"Oh," Molly said, and realized that maybe she had—the day of the ultrasound, wasn't it? When she and Tate were both so happy and everything had seemed as though it was working out fine...

Donetta continued expressing her outrage. "How could he kick you out when you're having *twins?*"

Molly considered telling Donetta that Tate hadn't exactly kicked her out, that she'd still be with him if only she'd opened her mouth and said *yes*. But if she told Donetta that, she'd be in for a thousand more questions and a butt-load of unwanted advice. Nope. Better to just sigh and nod and resist the urge to do more with her scissors than cut Donetta's hair.

If only she didn't miss him so darn much. If only she didn't feel as if a part of her was missing. If only she didn't wish every night that she could roll over and find him there, ready to wrap his big, strong arms around her and listen to her secrets and kiss her until her brain leaked out her ears.

If only she didn't find herself wondering constantly, where is he now?

What is he up to?

How is he doing? Is he all right...?

Tuesday afternoon around three, Tate sat at his desk, an open bottle of whiskey on the desk pad in front of him. The bottle blocked the center of his computer screen, which was showing him columns of numbers he didn't give a good damn about.

He set down his empty glass, picked up the bottle and tipped in another two fingers' worth. "Hidey-ho," he muttered. "Why stop there?" And he poured in two fingers more.

He knocked back about half of it and plunked his glass down—and noticed that Tucker was standing the doorway, a duffel in one hand and that ugly puppy of his in the other.

"Pitiful," Tucker said. "Not to mention classic."

Tate squinted at him—truth was, Tucker looked a little bit blurry around the edges. "I don' need to hear it—where you goin'?"

"Headin' out."

Tate squinted harder. "Leavin'?" He blinked and shook his head. There. Tucker was a little bit clearer. Wasn't he? "Uh...where to?"

"I've got a few things to take care of. Fargo and I'll be back in a day or two."

Tate considered asking him a second time where the hell he might be going—and if Leland knew that his new law partner was just taking off out of nowhere like this. But that was a lot of words and his tongue was feeling mighty thick.

"Do your liver a favor," Tucker said. "Call her. Tell her you can't live without her and you were a damn fool."

Before Tate could get his fat, slow tongue around *Go to hell,* Tucker had vanished from the doorway. A moment later, Tate heard the front door open and shut.

And a second or two after that, the alarm went off. Damn that brother of his, he hadn't bothered to deal with it before he went out the door.

"M'ranna!" Tate shouted. "M'ranna, the alarm!" He bellowed for the housekeeper a couple more times before it finally occurred to him that she had taken off to buy groceries about an hour before.

"T'rrific," he muttered, as the piercing screaming sound drove into his skull. Slurring every swearword he knew, one after the other, Tate fumbled with the combination lock in the bottom drawer of the desk. Finally, he got the damn thing open and reached in to pull out his trusty .38.

The alarm screamed on, drilling a hole of burning hurt into his pounding head. Still discovering new swearwords to slur, Tate pushed himself upright and staggered toward the unbearable sound.

Since the world was slowly spinning, he braced himself in the doorway Tucker had recently vacated and took aim, bracing his shooting arm with his free hand.

Two shots exploded, each to the accompaniment of the constant, screaming beep, each creating a mini-crater in the wall. On the third shot, he was more careful. He squinted down the barrel, ordering the world to stop moving, *willing* the damn bullet to go where he pointed it.

A hit!

The alarm box exploded—and sweet quiet reigned. Tate let his arm drop to his side and slid slowly down the door frame. He was still sitting there when the Tate's Junction two-man police department arrived.

"Lord in heaven, Tate," said Police Chief Ed Polk. "What's happened here?"

"Li'l dishcussion with the alarm, tha's all. An ish no pro'lem. Molly allus hated the damn thing, anyways…"

Drinking didn't help.

He realized that the next morning, when his head pounded like a gong and his stomach felt like it was lined with battery acid. He was just as miserable without Molly as he'd been before he got falling-down drunk. Only now, he was miserable *and* in excruciating pain.

The hangover passed. By Thursday morning, he was feeling almost normal again—or rather, as normal as it was possible for him to feel when the only woman for him had packed up and moved out of his life, taking their unborn babies with her.

By Thursday afternoon—four days, fifteen hours

and about twenty minutes after she left him—he was starting to admit a few scary things to himself.

He pulled a certain family album from a low shelf in the living room and went to his office, where he moved the big ottoman in the sitting area. Pushing the chairs out of the way, he flipped the rug back and opened the floor safe. From the safe he removed a document: the marriage license of Blake Phelan Bravo and Penelope Louise Tate. He put the rug back down and the chairs and ottoman in place on top of it and he went to sit at his desk, where he laid the document on the desk pad before him and opened the family album to the two pictures of his mother and father on their wedding day.

He looked at the pictures first, as he'd done a hundred times before. In both of them, his mother stared straight at the camera, wearing a deer-in-the-headlights look, as if she'd been caught standing next to this strange man and wasn't sure what price she would pay for it. His father looked at his mother in one picture—and off to the side in the other. In both he was turned three-quarters away, giving a great view of his ear and one side of the back of his head, but making it pretty difficult for someone who'd never known him to imagine what he'd actually looked like. He'd had dark hair and he was tall and broad-shouldered—like a fair percentage of men.

Tate put the album aside and studied the marriage license. He examined the signatures of his parents, looked at his mother's and father's birthdates, their residences at the time of the marriage, their years of education completed. There were the full names of both sets of parents—his grandmother and his grandfather and two other grandparents he'd never met. The license also had boxes for the occupations of his mother and father—hers, student; his, "investments." It had boxes for education completed and type of "business or industry."

There was a hell of a lot of information on a marriage license, Tate found himself thinking. Given that his father had filled at least some of the boxes with true information, there would definitely be enough on the document in front of him to find out for certain if the wild things his mother had written in that diary of hers might be true.

Tate leaned back in his chair and stared off toward the far wall. As he stared, he pondered.

Deep things. Scary things. Things he never would have admitted he'd *ever* considered in the past.

Things like how, just possibly, Molly was right about him being kind of screwed up on the subject of his father and his mother and what the hell really went on there.

Things like how, maybe, he had more of Ol' Tuck in him than he liked to think.

Things like how he never should have told her she had to marry him or go.

About then, at the very time he finally fully admitted that he had been a blind, stupid fool, the alarm box, fixed by a puzzled representative of the alarm company the day before, started blaring.

Figuring it had to be an intruder, Tate bent down to get his .38.

But before he got the lock open, Miranda trotted by the door, hurrying in from the back of the house. A moment later, the alarm quit bleating and he heard

Tucker say, "Thanks, Miranda. I hate that damn thing."

Miranda murmured something and passed Tate's line of sight a second time, headed back the way she'd come. Tate heard scrabbling noises and then Tucker's puppy appeared in the doorway. It dropped to a sitting position, whined once and then panted with enthusiasm, floppy pink tongue hanging out.

Tate was actually considering calling it over when Tucker finally came to the door and scooped it up. "Hey, big brother. Got someone I want you to meet."

Tucker stepped aside and Tate saw the guy with him. A tall guy, dark-eyed and broad-shouldered. Lean. Handsome, in a fine-featured kind of way. A stranger.

And yet, there *was* something familiar about him. Something in the set of the eyes and the shape of the face, in the full-lipped, sensual mouth.

It came to Tate. The guy looked a little like Tucker—and a little like the man Tate saw when he looked in the mirror.

By then, Tate was figuring it out.

It was only icing on the cake when Tucker said, "Meet our half brother, Marsh."

Tate might have been facing some tough facts about who he was and what was wrong with him. But he still had enough of Ol' Tuck in him to need at least a little confirmation.

He asked the stranger, "Do you know your father's middle name?"

Marsh nodded. "Phelan."

Tate looked at his father's name on the license in front of him: Blake Phelan Bravo.

It was enough. He stood and came around the desk, hand outstretched, to greet the half brother he'd never known he had.

Chapter Seventeen

Friday morning at ten, Molly had Emmie Lusk before her in the styling chair. After much agonizing and discussion, Emmie had decided to go from warm sable-brown to ash blonde.

Molly knew it was a mistake. Emmie's yellowish skin tone was going to look downright jaundiced with a bunch of ash-yellow hair all around it. She'd tried to steer Emmie to the warmer blond shades, at least. Emmie wouldn't be steered. And in the end, as a successful businesswoman, Molly understood that a service was a service and the customer had a right to get what she was willing to pay for.

In this case, for the chance to look like she'd come down with hepatitis B.

Molly was trying to focus on the bright side. Once she saw how awful the color was on her, Emmie would want a redo. And Molly would provide it, charging the usual rate. Win/win, as they say...

Win/win, Molly thought bleakly as she brushed on the color solution after lifting out the sable. Life was just a series of opportunities for everybody to get what they wanted, now wasn't it?

Hardly.

Tate, she thought, as she did about a thousand times every day. And, just like every other time, her stomach felt tight and there was an aching around her heart.

She was getting very close to doing what she'd never thought she'd do, because living this way, without him, well—it just hurt too much. So she was working up the courage to give it one more shot, though she knew that a man like Tate would never give second chances once he'd drawn the line.

Too bad. She was going to try, anyway. She was going to go see him, and she was going to tell him—

Molly never finished that particular thought. Because right in the middle of it, the bell rang over the door, and there he was.

Tate! Her heart raced faster and her hands started shaking.

"Tate," she whispered, and carefully set down the bowl of color solution and the solution brush. "Elise, honey, take over for me here," Molly said to one of the other stylists.

"Now, wait a minute," snapped Emmie. "I don't want just anyone fooling with my hair."

"Don't you worry, Emmie," Molly replied, taking off her Latex gloves and tossing them aside. "Elise'll fix you up fine..."

Whatever Emmie said next, Molly didn't hear it. She heard nothing, *saw* nothing, but the tall, broad-shouldered man who'd just come in the door.

Tate had looked over. He saw that *she* saw him. "Molly," he whispered. He spoke too softly for her to hear it, but she saw his lips form her name.

And she whispered back, "Oh, Tate…"

It was right about then that she registered the fact that he had someone with him, someone tall, dark-haired and broad-shouldered, just like Tate. The man wasn't as blunt-featured as Tate, but still, it seemed to Molly, there was a faint resemblance.

Her feet were moving, carrying her toward Tate. And Tate was walking straight toward her. He said, loud and clear that time, "Molly, I'd like you to meet my brother, Marsh Bravo."

And that was when she knew—that was when she allowed herself to believe that, just maybe, they would be all right.

They drove to the ranch house, the three of them: Molly, Tate and Tate's long-lost half brother. There was so much Molly needed to know and the proof, Tate said, was back at the house. That was fine with Molly. There was altogether too much gaping and whispering going on at the Cut, anyway.

By tomorrow, word about Marsh Bravo would be all over town—and about how Tate had come to get Molly, as well. Molly accepted that folks would talk. It was how things were when you lived in the Junction.

At the ranch house, Miranda had put out a mid-morning snack. They sat around the table in the breakfast room and Marsh and Tate showed her the proof of who their father had really been—the marriage license that matched up with what his mother had written and with what Marsh knew about the man who'd fathered both of them. Marsh said there were other brothers, three of them, in Nevada, just as Penelope had written. Marsh said he'd met them. Their names were Aaron, Cade and Will.

"And I'll bet," Marsh said to Tate, "that as time goes by, we're going to find out that you and Tucker and I and our Nevada half brothers aren't the only ones. Your mother wrote that he mentioned he had other families around the country. And I believe it. Our father lived in the rundown shack out in the woods where I grew up for thirty years. But he wasn't home much, you know? When I was a kid, he would be gone for weeks—sometimes even months—at a time. Nobody knew where he went when he took off. So there *could* be more of us. Knowing my father, I'd lay odds there are." Marsh had a wife and kids in Oklahoma. He said he hoped that soon his family would have a chance to meet his Texas brothers.

Eventually, Tucker came in with his new puppy, Fargo. Molly held the adorable funny-looking little critter and let him lick her face and Tate pretended he didn't approve.

"Oh, you know you want to hold him, too," she teased.

"Keep that damn dog away from me," he commanded.

Molly only laughed. She knew that sometime, when he thought no one was looking, he'd be reaching out to give Fargo a scratch behind his big, floppy ear.

"Come with me," he said quietly, a little bit later, when Tucker had taken Marsh out for a look around the property. He held out his hand.

Molly laid hers in it, the familiar rush of joy and heat bursting all through her just from his touch.

He led her upstairs, down the landing, and into the room that had been his mother's. Everything was just as she'd left it that awful day almost a week ago.

"This way." He pulled her into the big, bright, empty room that his mother had once called her studio. And right there, in the middle of the scratched, paint-spotted floor, he fell to his knees. "Molly..." He had to pause, to clear his throat.

She looked down at his beloved face and she ached for him. For a big, strong, handsome, rich guy, he sure did look scared. She reached down, put her hand against the side of his dear face. He caught it, pressed his lips to it.

"Molly," he said, his voice husky with emotion. "In the time you been gone, I've had to come to grips with a few things. The brother you just met is one of them, the truth about my father is another. The fact that it's damn likely my father had another wife already when he married my mother.... Molly, those are things that have rocked the foundation of the man I thought I was.

"But the biggest thing I learned, the most *important* thing, is the bald truth that I never should have pushed you into a corner the way I did. I was wrong to do that and, Molly, if you'll give me another chance, I will never do such a thing to you again.

Because, Molly, it's finally gotten clear to me that I can live without doing the right thing and marrying you easier than I can live without *you.* So, if you can't see your way clear to take my ring and my name, well, I hope you'll just stay with me, Molly. I hope in whatever way you can, you'll be mine. Because, damn it, I love you. My life is pure misery without you. You are the woman I want for the rest of my life. And however I can have you, I'll take you that way.''

Molly found that her legs didn't want to hold her up there, so high above him. She let them bend. Slowly she sank to her knees with him.

''Molly?'' he asked in a reverent whisper, his face full of hope and the beginnings of joy.

To Molly, right then, it seemed that the room grew brighter still. A golden, warm and magical light suffused it. Her eyes had teared up. Everything looked soft and bright and blurry.

''Oh, Tate. You mean it? You *love* me?''

Tate muttered something. Even as close as she was, with her hand in his, she couldn't make it out. But she was pretty sure it was a swearword. He demanded gruffly. ''Are you trying to tell me you didn't know?''

She pulled his hand close and kissed his knuckles. ''Well, Tate, you never said it.''

He gaped. ''I should have? I should have said it?'' Too moved to speak right then, she sniffed and nodded. ''Damn it, Molly. Why didn't you just tell me so?''

She laughed and the laugh kind of caught on a happy sob. ''Oh, Tate. I didn't know how bad I wanted to hear it—not till you said it. Besides, it only really counts if you think it up yourself. And, Tate?''

He touched her shoulder, lightly stroked her hair. ''Yeah?''

''Well, Tate. I love you, too. With all my heart and body and soul. I have loved you forever, I realize that now. Though the last thing I thought I'd ever do was admit it to you—*or* to myself.''

''Forever?'' His expression said that was a very long time.

She nodded. ''Since I was a little girl, and I'm not kidding. I'd see you in town and my heart would just... Oh, Tate. There are no words. And you never noticed me. Not until I ran for mayor.''

''I never thought I'd say it, but your running for mayor was the best damn thing that ever happened to me.''

''Oh, Tate. For me, too. And, Tate?'' She kissed his hand again and then tucked it up close, against her heart. ''I would be so honored. And so happy, if...well, if you would, um...''

''Molly,'' he said. He looked stricken, poleaxed, punched in the gut—as if he didn't quite dare to believe.

And she said it, she asked him, somehow she managed it. ''Tate. Please marry me. Be my husband. Let me be your wife. Let's...make a life together, as a family, with our babies. Oh, Tate. Will you do that? Will you marry me? Please?''

''Molly,'' he said again, and he reached for her. She swayed against him. His big arms closed around her. ''Molly, Molly, Molly...'' He bestowed a rain of kisses on her upturned face.

"Is that a yes?" she dared to ask.

"Yes," he growled.

And then he kissed her, long and deep.

They were married a week and a day later, on the last Saturday in August, out in Emigration Park, just as Dixie and Ray had done. Molly had both her mother and her grandmother for her attendants. Tate had Tucker for his best man. Marsh and his family came down from Norman and just about every citizen of Tate's Junction was there. No one wanted to miss the moment when Tate Bravo finally got Molly O'Dare to say "I do."

There was a deep and awestruck silence when the moment came at last.

Pastor Partridge asked, "Molly O'Dare, do you take this man, Tate Bravo, to be your lawfully wedded husband, to love, honor and cherish him, forsaking all others, for as long as you both shall live?"

Molly didn't falter. She looked up into the waiting eyes of the only man for her and she answered, "I do. Forever and ever. Tate Bravo, I do."

*　*　*　*　*

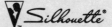

SPECIAL EDITION™

Coming in November to
Silhouette Special Edition
The fifth book in the exciting continuity

THE PARKS EMPIRE

DARK SECRETS. OLD LIES. NEW LOVES.

THE MARRIAGE ACT

(Silhouette Special Edition #1646)

by

Elissa Ambrose

Plain-Jane accountant Linda Mailer had never done anything shocking in her life—until she had a one-night stand with a sexy detective and found herself pregnant! *Then* she discovered that her anonymous Romeo was none other than Tyler Carlton, the man spearheading the investigation of her beleaguered boss, Walter Parks. Tyler wanted to give his child a real family, and convinced Linda to marry him. Their passion sparked in close quarters, but Linda was wary of Tyler's motives and afraid of losing her heart. Was he using her to get to Walter—or had they found the true love they'd both longed for?

Available at your favorite retail outlet.

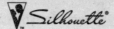

SPECIAL EDITION™

presents

bestselling author

Susan Mallery's

next installment of

Watch how passions flare under the hot desert sun for these rogue sheiks!

THE SHEIK & THE PRINCESS BRIDE

(SSE #1647, available November 2004)

Flight instructor Billie Van Horn's sexy good looks and charming personality blew Prince Jefri away from the moment he met her. Their mutual love burned hot, but when the Prince was suddenly presented with an arranged marriage, Jefri found himself unable to love the woman he had or have the woman he loved. Could Jefri successfully trade tradition for true love?

Available at your favorite retail outlet.

SILHOUETTE *Romance*®

Don't miss

DADDY IN THE MAKING
by Sharon De Vita

Silhouette Romance #1743

A daddy is all six-year-old Emma DiRosa wants.
And when handsome Michael Gallagher gets
snowbound with the little girl and her single
mother Angela, Emma thinks she's found
the perfect candidate. Now, she just needs
to get Angela and Michael to realize
what was meant to be!

Available November 2004

SPECIAL EDITION

#1645 CARRERA'S BRIDE—Diana Palmer
Long, Tall Texans
Jacobsville sweetheart Delia Mason was swept up in a tidal
wave of trouble while on a tropical island holiday getaway.
Luckily for this vulnerable small-town girl, formidable casino
tycoon Marcus Carrera swooped in to the rescue. Their mutual
attraction sizzled from the start, but could this tempestuous duo
survive the forces conspiring against them?

#1646 THE MARRIAGE ACT—Elissa Ambrose
The Parks Empire
Red-haired beauty Linda Mailer didn't want her unexpected
pregnancy to tempt Tyler Dalton into a pity proposal. But the green-
eyed cop convinced Linda that, at least for the child's sake,
a temporary marriage was in order. Their loveless marriage was
headed for wedded bliss when business suddenly got in the way
of their pleasure....

#1647 THE SHEIK & THE PRINCESS BRIDE—
Susan Mallery
Desert Rogues
From the moment they met, flight instructor Billie Van Horn's
sexy good looks and charming personality blew Prince Jefri
away. Their mutual love burned hot, but when Jefri was suddenly
presented with an arranged marriage, he found himself unable to
love the woman he had—or have the woman he loved. Could Jefri
successfully trade tradition for true love?

#1648 A BABY ON THE RANCH—Stella Bagwell
Men of the West
When Lonnie Corteen agreed to search for his best friend's long-
lost sister, he found the beautiful Katherine McBride pregnant,
alone and in no mood to have her heart trampled on again. But
Lonnie wanted to reunite her family—and become a part of it.

#1649 WANTED: ONE FATHER—Penny Richards
Single dad Max Murdock needed a quiet place to write and a baby-
sitter for his daughter. Zoe Barlow had a cabin to rent and needed
some extra cash. What began as a perfect match blossomed into the
perfect romance. But could this lead to one big perfect family?

#1650 THE WAY TO A WOMAN'S HEART—Carol A. Voss
Nan Kramer had lost one man in the line of fire and wasn't about to
put herself and her three children through losing another. Family
friend—and local deputy—David Elliot agreed that because of his
high-risk job, he should remain unattached. Nonetheless, David had
found his way into this woman's heart, and neither wanted to send
him packing....